WHERE THE SORREL ENDS

A NOVEL

NONA ME

NONA ME

To the school teachers of America.

We've entrusted to you the future of our nation, our society, our very civilization.

Thank you.

"The course of true love never did run smooth."

- Lysander, in *A Midsummer Night's Dream*, Act 1 Scene 1

CHAPTER 1

DAVID

June 3.

When I was a child, I spake as a child, I understood as a child, I thought as a child: but when I became a man, I put away childish things.

1 Corinthians 13:11

IT'S LOVELY UP HERE, among the grass and flowers and moss-covered walkways of this, our ancient hillside. The daylight's growing dim. A Pacific breeze slips through my thinning hair. The fiery sunset from only minutes earlier has all too quickly faded into the darkness of an unsympathetic sea.

Two fawns, not a hundred feet away, stand looking at me, ears erect, bodies taut, black noses twitching. I glance at my cell phone to check the time. Got to get this right.

It feels as though there's not another soul within a hundred miles; only the two of us. No one to disturb the agonized thoughts that course through my brain. No one to interrupt me when, a few minutes from now, I'll lower myself down from here, slipping onto my back, stretching myself out on the damp grass at my feet. But not yet. Not yet.

I'm sitting at my usual bench - the one upon which, over the past year, I've camped out, more than a hundred times, like some tragic, homeless figure. It's my favorite seat in all the world, notwithstanding the moss-covered slats, the powdery bird droppings, the rusty iron railings. There couldn't be a more picturesque place for the two of us to spend this precious time together.

The rhododendrons sway in the breeze, vibrant with color, fluttering on all sides like an army of purple-pink butterflies. They're in full blossom tonight, framed by the grand firs and Sitka spruces of the surrounding woodland.

The luminescent village which appears to lie just beyond the patch of lawn in front of my feet is picture-perfect against the dying purples and orange-reds of the western sky, a postcard view from a hundred years ago. The nineteenth-century steeples, the gingerbread houses, the Victorian painted ladies that bat their eyes at each other from either side of Main Street. Picture-perfect.

Other than a drifting cloud here or there, it's a fairly clear night for this particular corner of California. This is the place which the locals, shunning the very urbanity which characterizes the rest of the state, lovingly refer to as the Lost Coast. The moon - is it waxing or waning? I never remember to keep track - has made its appearance above the horizon. The first stars of the evening, Venus and Jupiter, are already winking above the shadowy trees.

Yesterday was the last day of school. I'm glad. I am *so* ready for summer break. And for wherever life takes me, after that. I'm feeling restless, I'll admit. Been that way for some time now. Like somehow I'm so very far from home, even though I actually live only a few miles up the road.

Here I sit, caught up in my despondency. Just myself and my sweetheart. The love of my life. The woman of my dreams.

I can think of not a single thing that remains to be discussed between her and me, so I maintain the silence, lost in the solitude of my thoughts, glad not to be interrupted by anyone or anything in the serenity of the moment.

I glance in her direction, then turn again to the sea, thinking back on my life, and hers. Running my mind for the thousandth time through the twisted maze of choices and events and circumstances that led the two of us inexorably to this precise spot. To this place of seclusion and beauty, where we find ourselves on this melancholy evening. Because at any given point in someone's life, the place in which that person finds himself or herself at that particular moment is simply the inevitable culmination of the ebb and flow of life's vicissitudes and fortunes.

To UNDERSTAND my story you'll need to know two things about me: First, I'm a bit obsessive, or maybe just superstitious. Probably both. Mostly with regard to recurring traditions, linked to dates on the calendar. I make no apology for this. I am, admittedly, a lifelong observer of certain specific, annual rituals.

The second thing to know about me is that, in my heart, I will forever be a hopeless romantic. Even as I write these words, allowing my thoughts to drift back to some of the idiosyncratic choices made in my youth, I smile as I catch myself emitting a long sigh . . .

~

WHEN I WAS EIGHT, my pet rat succumbed to the ravages of a cancerous tumor. I was devastated.

Every day after school I'd come home and spend hours with Pinqui: building mazes for him out of wood blocks; letting him run through the grass as he explored the periphery of the backyard; lifting him up along the railing of our wooden fence; balancing him on my head and laughing as he hesitated to climb down; tossing him out of my treehouse strapped to a large parachute, made of taped-together garbage bags, securely harnessed to his torso.

I used to let him wriggle through my jeans, slipping him inside through the top of my pants and feeling him crawl down my legs, his scratchy claws tickling me so agonizingly that sometimes I had to stamp my foot to get him down more quickly. Until one day I stomped without realizing he'd already reached the bottom. I crushed his rubbery tail under the heel of my tennis shoe. The smashed tail was bleeding severely. I thought the world had ended.

"Lo siento!" I cried, almost screaming, kissing his furry forehead in desperation, swearing to never again cause him to crawl down inside my pants. (As a child, I was in the habit of speaking in Spanish only to my rat and to my parents, though my folks' English was more than passably good. My own bilingualism notwithstanding, I never spoke in Spanish to anyone else. English was the language of choice for me.)

"No lo quise hacer. Te lo juro. *Tanto* lo siento, Pinqui!" I didn't mean to do it, I swear. I'm *so* sorry.

I was emphatic in the desperate apologies I uttered on that tragic day. But it didn't matter. The severed tail never grew back. It turned purple within a few days, then brownish-gray, finally falling off altogether, leaving only a stub. My beloved pet had been saddled with a permanent disability for the rest of his life, due entirely to my frivolity.

His name was derived from the color of his eyes, as well as of his nose and feet. His full appellation was, formally, *Pinqui El Rosado de Lopez-Mendoza*, incorporating the surnames of both my father and mother.

He was a white laboratory rat, and I grew increasingly concerned when I noticed a large lump forming in front of his chest that summer, a week before the new school year had begun.

"No hay nada que se puede hacer," my mother told me gently, brushing away the tear on my cheek. "Te vas a tener que preparar emocionalmente, mijo." Prepare yourself emotionally, my son. There's nothing we can do.

Her advice was timely, and yet, on that Saturday morning in mid-October when I discovered my pet's body, stiff and cold in the back of the cage, I was nonetheless devastated. I'd been praying for him to make it through. Desperately pleading with God to spare his life. Hoping against hope for a miracle. A miracle which never came.

This is not to suggest that God is, in principle, opposed to the granting of miracles to distraught children. Rather, in His wisdom, He deemed that it was best in this case that this particular prayer not be answered. At least not in the way I had hoped. Had the rat survived the cancer, it would inevitably have died anyway, sometime in the coming months. The lifespan of such creatures is roughly two years, after all. If the Good Lord were to spare the life of my pet each time I asked Him to, the highly unnatural result would be that the rat would still be with me today, and almost as old as I am. Not a particularly savory thought.

Though hard for me at the time, I now can see the wisdom of allowing Pinqui to die when he did. In fact, with the benefit of hindsight, I can understand why God allows all of us to die, sooner or later. Even those we love most of all.

I scratched my beloved rodent's name, together with the words "MAY HE REST IN PEES," all in capital letters, into the plank-wood siding of my backyard fence. An enduring personal trait that characterized my grade school years was the consistently atrocious quality of my spelling. At any rate, after writing the above inscription on the fence, I raided my dad's pile of broken bricks to construct a three-foot pyramid, in Pinqui's honor, beneath the epitaph. That monument of bricks remained in place throughout my childhood years, though the words on the fence faded away when the following spring arrived.

The remarkable thing is that from that day to this, once a year on October 19 at exactly 7:30 AM, I've faithfully observed a moment of silence for Pinqui. I've never once missed the date. It's quirky, I know. I'm a grown man. Old enough to understand that my long-dead rat neither knows nor cares that I continue to set aside time each year to remember him. But even as I write this, there isn't a doubt in my mind, but that I'll continue to maintain the tradition until the year I die. A bit obsessive-compulsive, as I said before. So shoot me.

Two years after my summer with Pinqui, I was a ten-year-old scamp with a raging crush on a freckle-faced girl named Kathleen, who lived across the street and down one house.

Not once did I speak to her, not even to say, "hi." I had no idea what she thought, or what her family was like, or even which teacher she had at school. She wasn't overly comely, and I only saw her from time to time, in the lunchroom or down a hallway. Always from a distance.

But none of that stopped me from fantasizing, day after day, when I came home from school and played on my swing set and ran through the yard like a wild animal. I was *Armstrong*, the world's toughest superhero, always finding myself confronting a newly urgent need to rescue Kathleen, invariably from some malefactor who would tie her up and treat her with gross cruelty. I would picture her in my mind, quietly crying, begging for help, and then I'd burst in on the bad guys, wiping them out with my superior skills before gently untying and releasing the pathetic, sobbing maiden.

Even at that tender age I wasn't too young to understand that it was all fantasy. Just a game. Yet it stirred feelings deep within me in a way that no TV show or movie ever could.

"Offer her something," my older brother proposed, one sunny morning. "Some kind of gift. A token of your affection."

"A *token*?" I asked. "What's a token?"

He rolled his eyes and left the room.

Later that same day, as if Mike's suggestion had been prophetic, I happened upon a discarded flask of perfume on my way home from school. The slender bottle was elegantly curved, sort of like a lopsided hourglass, with a push-down spray nozzle on the top. I'd found it lying there half-empty, on the sidewalk. I took it home and cleaned it up, adding enough water to fill it to the top.

The fact that it didn't look new, and that the contents were diluted, didn't trouble my adolescent designs in the least.

In my zeal I covered the bottle with a big piece of leftover wrapping paper displaying a group of Christmas penguins in various guises. I applied copious amounts of scotch tape. Then I penned an anonymous love letter, with an asymmetrical heart sketched in the middle:

To my deer Cathaleene,

May you always smell cleen.

Giv yourself a little spray

Maybe once or twice a day.

I'm giving you this purfyume

For you to keep inside your room.

But I feel to much shame

To tell you whats my name.

Sorry.

I PREPARED to insert this prose into an envelope with "Cathaleene" scrawled across the front. First, though, I doused the envelope and my letter in a heavy cloud of perfume. Enough came out after several sprays to saturate not only the envelope and the wrapping paper, but also my hands, the desktop, and a couple of spare sheets of stationery paper as well.

After spending the better part of an hour trying to work up the courage to deliver the missive, I finally forced myself to cross the street, sneaking onto Kathleen's front porch, placing the letter and the gift at the foot of her door. I rang the bell, dashed back across the street, and dove for cover behind some bushes in my front yard.

Kathleen herself opened the door, looking all around because, of course, no one was there. She stooped down and picked up the gift and the letter, a look of surprise on her face. Taking another quick glance from side to side, she disappeared inside the house. And that was that. Anticlimactic.

I never found out what she thought of the present, or if she ever even used the perfume. It didn't matter. Oh, the vicarious thrill I got, just knowing that her fingers were likely touching the very bottle I had touched! Her cute little freckled nose was smelling the same scent I had inhaled. The skin of her wrists and neck might become the secret places onto which my love offering would soon be sprayed. So exciting.

Crouching there behind the bushes moments after she'd gone back inside, I sensed that the poet within me was awakening. My eye had caught a brief yet poignant glimpse of that budding maiden's freckled visage, concurrent with a surge in my adrenaline and a noticeable thumping in my chest. This cocktail of emotions and physiological responses stirred my preadolescent soul. Writing became the logical and immediately accessible outlet for the emotional outpouring that threatened to spill over the embankments of my ten-year-old heart.

I dashed into the house and composed an impromptu essay onto the sheet of paper on the desktop, the one which had unintentionally been soaked in Kathleen's perfume:

TODAY I DEELIVRD a botl of purfyume to Cathaleene. She livs across the street. I was to scared to giv it to her myself. I rang the dorebel and just ran away.

She's pritty. Sumtimes I say hi to her.

My life will never be the same, becuz of her. I think I love her, maybee. She will never no it. No one will ever no it.

I'm only ten. Everyone tells me it wil take forever for me to be all growed up and everything. I know. I know.

But my life will never be the same, thanks to you, Cathaleene. I will alwees think of you. Even wen I'm a hundrd yeres old. I'll stil remember.

Thank you for making me fill this way.

Love David.

I SIGNED and dated the heavily-scented note, folding it over and over on itself until it formed a tiny square, inserting it into one of the baby food jars my mom had been saving for thumbtacks and pins. I screwed the lid on tight, grabbing a hand shovel from my dad's potting shed. Then I jumped onto my bike, baby food jar in tow. My destination was the Banning Museum park, only a few blocks from my home in the Wilmington district of Los Angeles.

Upon arriving and making sure no one was watching, I selected the most obscure corner I could find, behind a big tree, proceeding to dig a narrow, deep hole in the lawn, against the base of the wooden fence. I buried the jar, carefully replacing the dirt and sod, making it look like no soil had been disturbed there.

It's been many years since I've been back to that particular spot. But I'm fairly certain that even now I could still find the place where the jar's located. I doubt anyone has had reason to excavate there, from that day until this.

The promise I made to my ten-year-old self as I returned home on my bike that day, was that if I should indeed live to be a hundred, I would make a point of returning to the location with a shovel to dig up the jar, buried so many years ago. The time capsule from my first unrequited love.

Life went on after that, as it always does. I soon got distracted and lost all interest in Kathleen. I even began to grow embarrassed, at school, that she might someday guess my identity, and realize what I'd done. I tried to avoid running into her, averting my eyes rather than saying anything whenever she walked by. I began to regret having given her the bottle and the letter, vowing never to repeat so foolish an act in the future.

But my memory of the jar I buried in that park remains to this day. And every now and again I picture myself, as a hundred-year-old man, bending over the soil under those ancient trees, digging up the long-lost relic from my youth, a veritable buried treasure, smiling as I open the lid, holding it to my nose to inhale the ninety-year-old air, reliving the excitement and wonder and magic of what it was like, once, to be ten.

THE SUMMER after that brought a road trip, rare for our family, because my mother had an aversion to travel, finding it far too stressful for her tastes. She opted to stay home from this particular vacation, but my dad had Mike and me skip school on the last day of class, taking us all the way from Wilmington to Ft. Bragg, a ten-hour drive, where we stayed in a low-cost motel near the coast. The next morning we got up early and headed two-and-a-half hours further north, up the 101, until we turned off from the main highway and eventually came to that interminable concrete span known as *Fernbridge*, crossing over the foggy bed of the Eel River, and from there into a place that looked like we'd entered a fantasy world. We slowly made our way through downtown Ferndale, and though I was tired from the long drive, I couldn't keep from looking at the fairy-tale houses and storybook buildings along the way.

Just south of town we headed down a narrow country lane where it squeezed itself into a tiny valley between dense forests on either side, pulling into the driveway of a farmhouse belonging to my dad's favorite companion from the time he'd been a missionary, so many years before, in Japan.

The Garcias were a friendly family - Jaime, the smiling father, who immediately began to reminisce with my dad about their time together in Kyoto; Connie, an eleven-year-old like me with straight black hair, pulled into a pony-tail; and her two younger brothers, Freddie and Carlos, neither of whom could properly pronounce the letter "r."

I sat politely with Mike on the living room sofa, trying to grasp the conversation between the two men, failing miserably. The other kids had already given up and left, and my brother was yawning and nodding, leaning sideways onto the couch, mere seconds from hibernation.

Jaime and my dad were rambling on about experiences they'd had and people they'd met, at times laughing out loud together. The discussion between them was mostly in English, with Spanish words and phrases thrown in here and there for added color or emphasis.

Bored, I looked around the room, taking in the sights: shelves of books, mostly religious; time-worn family photos on the walls; an upright Kawai with a mismatched bench and a chipped bust of Chopin on top; a statue of Jesus with his arms outspread, the nail prints visible in his palms.

I felt a tap on my shoulder and turned to see the three kids motioning for me to follow. My dad seemed either not to notice or not to care, so I followed the girl and her brothers down the stairs into an orange-carpeted family room bursting with board games, Hot Wheels tracks, boxes of toys, a pile of building blocks, and thousands of scattered Legos pieces. Paradise.

The four of us worked together to construct an elaborate city of pillows, couch cushions, sheets and blankets. We played for hours, becoming instant best friends the way only young kids can.

I was having the time of my life when Mike yelled down from upstairs, calling for us to come up, for lunch. Quesadillas, drizzled with Tapatío sauce, with rice, beans and corn tortillas on the side. Heaven.

It was a nice day outdoors, so after lunch we bounced on the tramp for some time, then swung ourselves on the swing set and plopped down together in the sandbox, which, unfortunately, we found to be full of cat poop.

"Come on!" said Connie, running toward the woods at the edge of the yard. Freddie and Carlos, her brothers, followed along with us until we reached the creek. Connie crossed it easily, nimbly stepping on a grouping of flat stones. I crossed over after her, but the two boys remained behind. Too young.

Connie led me along a narrow yet well-worn trail, up the steep hillside behind her house, to a vantage point with a view of the tiny valley below. I was out of breath.

"This is nice," I said. "I guess we'd better be getting back."

"Nah," she said. "Dinner's not gonna be for hours. We've got lots of time. Come on. I wanna show you some stuff."

She headed further along the trail. I was hesitant.

"Isn't your dad gonna be worried?"

"You kidding?" she said, laughing. "I come out here all the time. Every single day, when it's summer. Even when it's raining. Sometimes I'm gone from home for the whole day. My dad doesn't care. Only thing he says is for me to stay on the trail, so I won't get ticks. Or poison oak. It's a lot safer out here than in the big city, anyway. That's where you come from, right? The big city?"

"I guess so," I said. "It's called Wilmington. Doesn't seem so big to me. But it's not like this place, *at all*."

I was following her down the trail, pushing aside the pine branches that overhung our route, as we talked. She turned off onto a side path, and after dropping into a ravine and crossing another creek, the way ahead of us branched off into three separate directions. We bore left. She knew where she was going.

"Look!" she said, reaching for something yellow on a mossy log along the side of the creek. She scooped the thing onto her finger – sticky, squirming, completely alien. To my eye, it looked exactly like what she said it was - a banana slug. We found a dozen more, along with two slow-crawling newts, bright red with their little grasping fingers, and a miniature dell where the creek water cascaded over a four-foot waterfall into an algae-covered pond, surrounded by ferns.

Connie took me to different spots where she'd hidden various things throughout this amazing stretch of woods, her own private forest: a dollhouse with six Barbies in it; a wooden box with hinges, filled with paper and colored pencils and a sharpener; a partially-covered cave into which she'd placed two plastic chairs and a small table with a chess set; a hidden rope swing which took us soaring out over the creek; a small enclosure where she kept a stack of metal pie pans for gold panning; a crude treehouse, with a box of rusting nails and some rotting scrap lumber and a couple of hammers, in case we wanted to do some building.

Dinner that night was better, even, than lunch had been – hot *pozole* with shredded lettuce and radishes on top, with a mug of thick *atole con canela* for each of us, and a square of flan for dessert. Jaime Garcia, fat and good-natured, most definitely loved to cook.

Mike and Connie and I sat around the kitchen table playing board games, munching on popcorn and drinking Seven-Up until late in the night, long after our fathers had gone to bed. When Mike finally yawned and got up to leave, Connie headed toward the deck in back.

"Come here," she whispered to me, and I stepped outside with her. I was surprised at how bright the stars were in the sky. Where I lived in the L.A. basin, there was almost constant smog, or cloud cover.

"That's Orion," she said, pointing out the most obvious constellation to me. "Those three stars are his belt. He's a hunter."

"Orion," I repeated.

"And over there is *Ursa Major*. The big dipper. See it?"

We stood out there for fifteen minutes as she pointed out every constellation to me, giving me the background stories on the gods and goddesses and signs of the zodiac that they represented.

I slept that night in a sleeping bag on the floor downstairs, next to my brother.

The following morning we ate *huevos rancheros con chorizo* for breakfast, and then my dad took Mike and me on a trip around town and to the beach, to see the sights.

We were back with the Garcias in time for lunch, after which Connie showed me that she'd packed two Tupperware containers with food for her and me to eat, for dinner. She explained, as we headed together into the forest, that she'd already obtained permission from both dads for us to stay out until the time that I had to leave – 9 p.m.

"Today," she said, turning back to smile at me as we made our way up the hill, "I'm going to show you my biggest secret of all. I've never told anyone about it. You're the only one, besides me, who's going to know. But you have to promise to keep it a secret."

"Ok," I said. "I promise."

She looked doubtful.

"That wasn't much of a promise."

"What do you mean?" I asked

"I mean, a real promise has to be strong. Like you mean it. Like you're really going to do what you say."

"Ok," I said. "I'll try again. I promise not to tell anyone about your secret. Even though I don't know what it is."

I looked at her for approval, but she was frowning.

"Or else what?" she asked. I was confused.

"I mean," she said, "what are you going to do, if you don't keep your promise?"

"Oh," I said. "If I don't keep my promise, I'm going to . . . eat a banana slug."

She started to laugh.

"Sounds good," she said. "Now I believe you. Come on. This way."

She darted off ahead and I had to run to keep up. We seemed to keep going forever, from one obscure trail to the next, over logs, around boulders, past ancient Sitka trees with trunks as big as houses. Finally she slowed down, coming to a stop before a downward slope in the trail. I tried to see what was up ahead, but the undergrowth was too dense.

"Close your eyes," she said.

I complied, taking a deep breath.

Then I felt her hand slip into mine, gently pulling, leading me down the incline. I hadn't been expecting that. My breathing sped up.

"Careful now," she cautioned. "We're almost there."

I opened my eyes for a split second, taking a quick peek, not to see the place to which she was leading me, but to look at her hand, to see what it looked like, holding mine. I'd never held hands with a girl before. It felt nice. Warm. I liked it.

"Ok," she said, letting go. "You can open them now."

I blinked once or twice. We were standing above a tiny indentation in the hillside, a miniature dell, formed by a ravine that was capped on both ends by rocks and brush, surrounded by trees so densely bunched around it that I couldn't see into it. The place was so well hidden that unless a casual passerby like me knew to look for it, he would likely walk right past it without ever knowing it was even there.

I turned and looked behind us, to see the way we'd come. There was a tiny path, only slightly worn, winding through an ocean of green sorrel along the forest floor. The sorrel seemed to stretch on forever, beneath the trees. Turning back around to face the tiny basin in front of us, I saw that we'd arrived at the very edge of the sorrel carpet through which we'd traveled. Between us and the dell stood nothing more than some large rocks and a thicket of gigantic ferns.

We climbed down a set of naturally-formed steps in the rock, leading us into the small hollow below. A partition of western sword ferns blocked the way, and it was impossible to move forward without squeezing through the narrow gap between them. They were dripping with dew. I nonetheless brushed past, getting my face and upper body wet in the process.

Emerging with Connie onto the other side, I gasped, my eyes wide in wonder.

Directly in front of us, completely sheltered and concealed by the dense brush above us on all sides, was a small grassy clearing, in the middle of which stood a modest log cabin, perhaps a hundred years old, with a large stone fireplace on one end. The old roof was sagging, covered with moss, and one of the walls on the back side had a big hole in it and was starting to fall down. But the rest of the structure was intact, though it was missing a door. The windowpanes had long since been broken.

"Wow," was all I could say. "Does anyone else know about this?"

"No one in the world. Come inside. You'll see. I don't think anyone's been in it for a hundred years."

There was something magical about the old place. The original occupants had left some of their possessions behind – bits of broken china, a couple of musty grammar books which were about to fall apart, a headless baby doll, a rusty iron poker by the fireplace, a warped table that was missing one leg, a pot-bellied stove, covered in rust.

My sense of exploration led me to search all around the area, inside and outside of the structure, hunting for signs of civilization, searching for clues to the past, like an archaeologist. It was wonderful.

Then, without planning it out beforehand, Connie and I fell into a game together, in the most natural way. I took on the role of papa and she was the mama.

We played house, for more than an hour. We pretended that we were the original settlers who'd built the cabin, a century ago. Connie worked in the garden, tended the chickens, taught our children their readin', writin' and 'rithmatic. I went and worked in the fields, plowing, harvesting, chaining up the horses. We ate a pretend dinner together, with our imaginary kids, at the big table, after which we sat as a family and read some verses from the bible. Then we put the children to bed, sitting together by the fireplace, enjoying each other's company.

It was all pretend. Only make-believe. And it was a girl's game, I thought, not a boy's. Looking back I can see how overtly sexist it all was, assuming the woman's place to be not in the workforce but at home, washing and scrubbing and cooking and cleaning in a subservient way, seemingly for the sole benefit of her pampered husband.

In spite of that, I had never in my life been so completely enthralled as I was that afternoon with Connie, in our hidden cabin out in the middle of nowhere. I didn't want our game to end. I kept inventing new angles, new wrinkles in the evolving storyline, new ways to keep the play going.

"Jenny," I said, using Connie's made-up character name, "I don't mean to frighten you, darling, but you ought to know that I saw bear tracks last night."

"No!" Connie said, feigning fear. "Not near the cabin, I hope?"

"Just beneath yonder window," I said, pointing.

She pretended to be deeply worried.

"Well Johnny," she said (Johnny was the name of my character), "what do you recommend I do? What if you're out working in the field and that big old bear comes back?"

"I reckon," I said, trying to affect a country accent, "if it does come back, it'll be on account of your excellent cooking. Now, you're gonna have to make a choice, darling. Either you feed the beast, or you smack it on the head, as hard as you can, with your cast-iron skillet."

We laughed, and then Connie said suddenly, out of character, "I'm hungry."

We opened the lunchboxes she'd packed, enjoying together a simple repast of cold tortillas, cheese slices, a couple of mealy apples, two bags of Fritos chips, a homemade cinnamon roll for each of us, and a pair of pop-top cans of bean dip. It was the most delicious meal I'd eaten in my life.

After we were full we sat and talked, about everything under the sun. Connie was neither quiet nor reserved; she was full of opinions, and only too happy to share them. She also had a great sense of humor, and a twinkle in her eye whenever she told a joke.

We talked about her family – her brothers, her dad, and her mother in Arcata, whom she visited for an hour or two, every other weekend. Her parents had been separated for more than three years, with no indication that they'd ever be getting back together. But Connie didn't seem to mind. Her mom had gone through manic-depressive extremes all of her adult life, generally refusing to take medication for it. Very hit or miss. Though Jaime and the kids loved her, it was almost impossible to live with her.

She got me to talk about my own home life – my dad, my brother Mike, my mom, who hated to travel. I told her about my life in the L.A. area – the gangs, the drugs, the culture, the violence.

After a while I went outside, shouldering a big stick like it was a rifle, pretending to hunt for something, for dinner. When I came back into the cabin Connie was standing there impatiently, stamping a foot restlessly, looking like she'd been waiting forever for me to come home.

"*There* you are," she said, acting as though she was upset that I'd been gone for so long. In reality, I'd only been outside of the cabin for about ten minutes. "I've been waiting for you to get home, honey. Come over here."

She raised her arms and held them out to me, as if to give me a hug, her foot still stamping the ground impatiently, demandingly.

It was all pretend, anyway. Just a role-playing game. So I acted like it was an everyday thing as I stepped casually into those outstretched arms and gave a quick squeeze, releasing her promptly and taking a few steps back, not wanting to allow things to become uncomfortable between us. I'd been having too much fun, for the game to suddenly end in awkwardness or something. Better just to play along and not make a big deal of it.

She sat down and pretended to be rocking the baby and tending the fire after that, as we talked about our plans for the future, our favorite novels and movies, our musical tastes, our friends at school. I tried to keep my mind from wandering back to the fact that this attractive girl had just given me a hug. The first time I'd ever been hugged by a girl. And I'd liked it.

After a while I could see that it was beginning to get dark outside. I tried to be subtle as I checked my watch. No luck. She noticed.

"We have to be back by nine," I said, as though she hadn't already known. She said nothing, only looking at me with a bit of a frown. Then she abruptly got to her feet and headed toward the fireplace, grabbing a stick from the floor, pretending to stir a pot of make-believe stew.

"Johnny," she said, her back to me, "I do declare that this time I've spent with you, living in this cabin of ours, raising our young brood, has been the happiest time of my life." She set the stick down, keeping her back to me.

"Careful," I said to her. "If you don't pay attention to what you're doing, you're liable to burn the stew."

She turned with a puzzled look on her face, and I pointed to the stick she'd been holding. She snickered and picked it up again, once more making her stirring motions over the imaginary stewpot.

"Now, don't you go worrying your head over *that*, darling," she said over her shoulder. "I've made many a batch of stew in my time. Never once have I burned it."

"There's a first time for everything," I said, remembering one of my mother's adages, trying to sound serious, wrinkling my nose and sniffing the air as though the dinner had already been spoiled. "The kids will surely starve, tonight. But at least we can set the stewpot outside. For the bear."

She laughed out loud, but I glanced again at my watch. I knew how angry my dad could get, when I was late for things. Sometimes he hit me. I didn't think he was going to do that this time, at least not in front of the Garcias, but I wasn't anxious to take the risk. I took a step toward the cabin door.

"Wait!" said Connie. I was surprised to catch the merest hint of desperation in her voice. "Not yet."

It was hard to be sure in the diminishing daylight, but I thought her eyes were shining, just a bit. Was it possible that she'd been *crying?*

"I don't want you to go," she said simply, her voice solemn, husky. She swiped at one of her eyes with a shirt sleeve, not looking at me.

I felt warm all over. Somehow this skinny little girl, whom I'd only met the day before, had become my best and most important friend in the world. Wilmington seemed oceans away. She turned to look at me then, her face dark with apprehension.

My mind experienced a sudden clarity. There was no thought in my head, other than the right there and the right then – that dilapidated old cabin with its half-caved-in roof. The enchanting girl who stood inside it, by the crumbling fireplace, staring at me through pleading eyes.

I walked over to where she stood, looking into her face, not sure what to do next. She turned away, embarrassed, acting like she was straightening things up, dusting the imaginary furniture.

"When we get married," she said without looking at me, and I knew she was no longer pretending, "we're going to have six kids. Three little girls. Three boys. And you're going to build a house for us, just like this one. Only it'll be new. And nice. And I'll have my sewing table, right over there."

She pointed to the corner farthest from the fireplace.

"We'll keep the dishes in a china cabinet, just about here," she said, stepping to the side, indicating a wall. "I *like* china cabinets."

I nodded.

"You'll have a good job," she went on. "So will I. We'll keep the house neat and tidy, working together, side by side. We'll raise the children, you and I. Together. Teach them to love themselves. And to love the Lord. They'll grow to be tall and strong. And good."

She took a few steps in my direction, not looking directly at me, still rambling on about our future together.

"We'll be needing a big barn, of course. Horses. And a tractor to plow the fields. Maybe a cow. Some chickens. But no pigs. Please – no pigs."

I smiled.

"I'll be the one to get the kids ready for school every morning," she went on. "You'll make sure they always do their chores."

She was standing close to me, talking breathlessly, chattering about her plans for our future together. She stepped even closer. I could smell her. It made me awkward and uncomfortable. I had to close my eyes for a moment. But I stood my ground.

"And you'll come home at night," she continued, her voice low and sultry, "after a long day at work. Dirty and tired. And *I* will have been working, too. Maybe I'll have a career, like yours. Or maybe I'll just have been home with the kids all afternoon. I'll be tired. No question about that. But it won't matter. I'll bring you your supper, and a stool to prop your feet on. And you'll bring nice things home for me, too. Maybe you'll massage my tired back. And you'll ask me how my day went."

Her voice was soft, her eyes intoxicating. I couldn't look away.

"And then," she whispered, "after it gets dark outside, we'll tuck the kids into their beds. And we'll sit by the fire together, just you and I. When everything outside is completely still. And quiet. We'll talk over our plans for the coming day. I'll look at you. And you'll look at me. And then . . . then . . ."

She stopped talking. I held my breath. She was inches away, looking up into my eyes. I swallowed.

Ever so slowly, not taking her eyes from mine, she reached her hands forward, fingers extended, covering my ears with her palms. I could no longer hear the outside world. Her touch felt warm, disorienting, gentle. Her fingertips curled gently behind my ears, cupping them in her hands. Slowly, deliberately, she drew my face to hers.

I knew what was coming. I was powerless to stop it.

The kiss felt soft, warm. Natural. Familiar, as though we'd done it lots of times before. It wasn't intense, or forceful, or full of pressure or desperation. Instead it just felt . . . right. Comfortable. Perfect.

It was only brief. She stood there looking at me afterward, awkwardly. Embarrassed. Shy.

I broke the ice by moving forward, grabbing her firmly around the waist, hugging her tightly to my body. I couldn't help it.

She closed her eyes and sighed, leaning her head into my shoulder. I could feel her breath on my neck. I was sure I'd died and gone to heaven.

"I love you," she whispered into my ear. "My heart belongs to you, David Lopez. It always will."

"I don't care if my dad hits me when we get back," I whispered. "It'll be worth it, just to spend a few more minutes here. With you."

When I'd said that, a spark of recognition and concern flared in her eye.

"No," she said, moving away from me. "We've got to head home. You'd better not be late. But first I need to do something. It'll only take a minute."

She selected a sharp rock from the floor and began to carve our names onto a heavy log along the back wall. When I saw what she was doing I picked up a rock of my own, to help her. Together we drew a lopsided heart, with an arrow poking through it, around our names, giggling at the artwork once we'd finished. She reached forward and added a plus sign between 'Connie' and 'David.'

After that her soft eyes looked into up into mine, and I thought I was going to melt into the ground, right there where I was standing. She took me by the hand again, and I found myself wishing she'd never let go.

I couldn't stop looking at her as we headed back toward her house. That skinny little silhouette of a girl, so pretty, holding my hand, leading me through the darkening woods. It was too dark to detect any green in the endless sorrel as we stepped along the narrow path, past the rocks and ferns that surrounded the tiny valley with the cabin. I felt no fear despite the shadows and unfamiliar terrain, but my heart was pounding away to beat the band, nevertheless. I wondered if she could feel the sweat on my hand.

As we made our way along the forest trails, I couldn't stop thinking about the kiss. The longer I dwelt on it, the more the impact of it grew, in my head. What had been a soft and intimate connection between us had escalated in my mind into an ecstasy of ardor and passion, increasing in intensity each time I replayed it in my memory. I began to wonder if we were going to kiss each other again, before the night was done. Should I stop her and whirl her around and lay a quick one on her? I utterly lacked the courage.

We continued to move along down the trail, under the light of the rising moon. All at once she stopped walking and turned to face me. My heart skipped a beat.

"I know you have to leave," she said. She was right. The motel room in Ft. Bragg, although guaranteed for late arrivals, was almost three hours away. "Nothing we say or do is gonna make our dads change their minds about that."

"I'll be coming back to Ferndale," I said, "Soon. To visit you." I tried to make myself sound more certain than I felt.

"Maybe," said Connie. "But once you get back to your city, your regular life, you'll probably forget. Not at first. But after a while. It's only natural."

"*Never*," I said, feeling more sure of the word than of any other I'd ever spoken in my life. "I will never forget you."

She smiled, but it was only a melancholy grin at best.

"I have an idea," she said, her eyes brightening, looking up into the clear sky. "What time is it?"

I looked at my watch, scratching my head, wondering what she was up to.

"9:12," I said.

"Ok." She started to walk again. "I want you to tell me when it's exactly 9:15, all right? I mean, *exactly*."

We moved along in silence, holding hands. I checked my watch every thirty seconds or so, until finally the time had come. I told her, and we stopped.

"Lie down," she whispered as she lowered herself to the ground.

I got down next to her, on my back, looking up through the tree branches, into the sky. I could feel her warmth as she pushed herself against my side, her head resting against mine, the loose strands of her hair tickling my neck. She raised a finger and pointed to a lone star which seemed to be off by itself.

"Do you see that one?" she said. "It's called Polaris. The North Star. Always pretty much in the same spot, year-round."

"Yeah," I said. "I see it."

"Ok," she said, clearing her throat, still looking upward. "Here goes. David Lopez, I, Connie Garcia, swear that every year, on this exact date, at precisely 9:15 p.m., I will lie down on the ground, wherever I am, and look up at the North Star for one solid minute, and think of you. Cross my heart, hope to die, stick a needle in my eye."

She turned and looked over at me. "Now you say it."

I closed my eyes.

"Connie Garcia. I, David Lopez, promise to lie down, wherever I might be in the world, at exactly 9:15 in the evening, and stare at Polaris for one minute, and think of you. On this date, every year, for the rest of my life. Cross my heart, hope to die. Poke a needle in my eye."

"9:15 California time," she said.

"9:15 California time," I repeated. We began to get to our feet.

"I hope you meant it," she said as we stood up together.

"Of course I did," I said.

"You'd better really do it, then," she said. "Every year, for the rest of your life. Just like you said. Because a promise is a promise."

"I will."

"No matter what?"

"No matter what."

"So will I."

"I know."

"And each time," she said, her voice a bit shaky, "when you look up into the sky on this day, you'll know that somewhere out there, I'm looking up into the same sky. Even if I'm on the other side of the country, or the world, or wherever. Anywhere. Even when I'm an old lady. I'll never forget. A promise is a promise."

There was a look of sadness in her eyes. I wanted to reassure her, to tell her I'd be back, to let her know that tonight was not going to be the end. But I said nothing.

"Your family might bring you back up here to visit again, someday," she said. "Maybe. Or maybe not. But no matter where you are, or where I am, at least once a year we'll have this time together, you and I. Our eyes will be looking at the same thing, at exactly the same time. And that way, at least for a minute or two, we'll be together again. And it won't make any difference where we actually are. We'll be together."

Our walk back to the house was entirely without conversation. At one point it sounded like she was sniffling a bit.

I didn't let go of her hand until we stepped inside, through the back door on the deck.

The two men were talking and laughing in the living room, but they were both on their feet, and when my dad saw me he pointed to his watch. I hurried to grab my stuff and load it into the car. He didn't seem to notice that I'd been holding Connie's hand. She only said two words to me as I slipped into my seat and reached to close the door: "Don't forget."

The drive back to our motel in Ft. Bragg was emotional, for me. I kept looking out my window into the night sky, searching for Polaris, re-committing myself to remain true to my promise, no matter what. I asked my dad at least half a dozen times to tell me when we might return Ferndale. He was non-committal.

"We'll see," was all he would say. "We'll see."

For the next two weeks I was a boy obsessed. My former after-school play acting, in which Kathleen had been my fantasy girl in distress, seemed utterly juvenile compared to what I'd experienced in Ferndale. I couldn't stop thinking about my magical time there, about all the things Connie had shown me, about how we'd pretended to be husband and wife.

Most of all I thought about our kiss, and how much it had come to mean to me. I yearned to hurry back to the northern coast, and wondered when I'd be able to go, and if she would still feel the same way about me when I got there.

It never occurred to my eleven-year-old brain that I might actually *do* something, like sitting down and writing her a letter, or even calling her on the phone. I suppose I was still bristling from the effects of having shared my feelings, in writing, with Kathleen, the year before. Besides, I knew I'd much prefer to *see* Connie in person, rather than merely writing to her. So instead of penning a letter, I mostly just pestered my dad about going back to Ferndale.

"We'll probably take another trip up there, next year," he would say.

But in the end, we never did.

WHEN THE SUMMER was nearly over I found that I was having trouble remembering specific details of what Connie looked like.

I started the sixth grade, and a girl named Eleni, with braces and black curly hair and a habit of gabbing with me about parties and Taco Bell and 'munchies,' sat in the seat in front of me. We became fast friends. It turned out to be an interesting semester.

By the time I turned twelve I'd almost completely forgotten about Connie, but one summer evening I happened to be reading something in a book about constellations, and I was reminded of the North Star, and of the promise I'd made. I kept telling myself every day during the first few days of June to be ready, and when the appointed night finally came, I slipped outside at 9:15 and lay down on the back lawn under a palm tree, staring up at the smoggy ceiling of gray above the city. It was impossible to see any stars, but I knew which direction was north, and I looked that way and remembered, and wondered whether Connie might be doing the same thing, lying on her back somewhere in Ferndale, looking up at the same spot in the sky, in that exact moment. Something told me that she was. It was difficult to explain or understand, but I could somehow sense her presence, even though she was hundreds of miles away. As though she were lying there on the grass, right next to me, looking up into the night sky, holding my hand.

Over the years, it's become a habit for me. Part of who I am. Never once have I missed the date, or forgotten. It's grown into a personal tradition, almost like a good luck charm, something I look forward to and count on each year. A tangible link to my past.

By the time I'd graduated from high school I had no memory of what Connie looked like, and only vague recollections of what we'd done and said to each other on that momentous weekend, so many years earlier. But the ritual of lying on my back and looking up at the North Star had by that time become firmly entrenched.

I remember Facebook-stalking her once, maybe ten years ago. I was curious to know what she'd done with her life. Who she'd become.

I couldn't find her.

I knew from that moment that she would continue to live on only in my mind, as a distant memory from my childhood. Something to commemorate, once a year. A happy past I could think back on, but never relive. One which would never again be part of my life.

∾

I LEARNED to play cello and auditioned my way to first chair in my high school orchestra cello section. I earned a black belt in taekwondo by my sophomore year. I was junior captain of the debate team the year we went to Sacramento to compete for the state title. We took third.

My parents got divorced that same year, after my mom, unwilling to put up with the abuse any longer, left my dad. I opted to go with her. Mike was already grown up by then, no longer living at home, so he didn't have to choose a side.

I certainly didn't want to keep living with Dad. There'd been plenty of violence directed toward me over the years, too, not only toward Mom. This in spite of the fact that Dad had been a church-goer all his life. I was ashamed of him after the acrimony and bitterness that came out during the divorce negotiations, making Mom cry herself to sleep at night, more than once. I dropped my dad's last name and started using Mom's as my own.

We bought a modest home in South Gate, and Mom and I stopped going to church. It wasn't a conscious choice; we just drifted into religious inactivity. Weekends offered tempting opportunities to relax and visit places and go shopping. Getting ourselves dressed for church on Sunday mornings became less and less convenient. More and more of a chore. My brother had long been a closet atheist all along, anyway, and Mom and I had mostly fallen out of contact with Dad, so our ties to the church were largely broken. Dropping our religion was surprisingly easy.

After I graduated I went on to UCLA, got my degree, and became an English teacher at a high school in San Pedro. It was a good career choice for me; I loved working with the kids, opening their minds to the wonders of great literature.

I married a girl named Sandy at twenty-six. We had two kids, a boy and a girl. Then one day my wife, whom I loved but not really, was standing next to the ironing board when she gave me a funny look and asked, "Did you hear that?"

"Hear what?" I said, buried deep inside my Saturday *New York Times* crossword, leaning back in the faux leather recliner that graced our tiny living room.

"It was weird. Like a popping noise. Inside my head."

She flashed me a strange smile, and her eyes rolled white. She collapsed onto the floor and was dead within twenty minutes. Sudden brain aneurysm.

I remarried at thirty-four. Becca, my second wife, was unable to get pregnant, a situation which resulted in nothing but heartache, stress and blame for both of us. We went to specialist after specialist; we tried everything, to no avail. I suggested adoption but she wouldn't hear of it.

It was ironic that she was so desperate to become a mother, because she left the raising of my own two kids entirely to me. I actually loved being a father, though, so it didn't ever become an issue. I gradually found myself spending more time with the children than with Becca.

The kids grew up, as children will do, and eventually flew the coop, making us empty nesters. Both of us had become, by this time, substantially overweight. Too many years of the Standard American Diet.

Our lives seemed to be missing something; we had no real sense of purpose. I was quite a bit north of three hundred pounds, and Becca wasn't far behind. I confronted her one morning and demanded that the two of us make some fundamental lifestyle changes. She agreed.

We joined Weight Watchers and stuck it out for a year. After that we tried various fad diets – Mediterranean, Paleo, colon cleansing, juicing. Always returning to our bad habits of binge-eating and high-carb comfort foods, between diets. A couple of human Yo-Yos.

A year later we made the drive to Blossom Bariatrics in Henderson, Nevada, to undergo gastric sleeve surgery together, after which we made ourselves stick to a strict whole-food-plant-based diet, losing all the excess weight we'd put on. Which was great, except instead of making us happier with our newly youthful bodies, it served only to instill in us the preoccupation that old age and senility were just around the corner. That we had to hurry and take advantage of any youthfulness we still enjoyed, before we lost it forever.

I took up karate again. Becca, who'd bought herself a completely new wardrobe and gotten her hair colored, ran off with some guy with tatts and earrings and a goatee who wore black leather and rode a big Harley.

I should've been hurt, but I wasn't. We'd stopped loving each other, years before. We completely fell out of touch after she took off. I never saw her again. Never wanted to. Didn't get around to filing the divorce papers for at least six months after she'd gone.

I underwent something of a midlife crisis of my own, after that. I was fifty-two then, more fit than I'd been for thirty years, pushing my physical limits in intense karate workouts every night, growing increasingly dismayed by the internal politics of the administrators at the high school in San Pedro. My dad had passed away a few years earlier, in the middle of my year of Weight Watchers. My mother, succumbing to end-of-life entropy in an assisted living center, had herself given up the ghost the previous spring. Mike and I had never been close, and he'd recently moved to Denver, with a family of his own. My ties to Southern California had never been more tenuous. Time to leave.

On a whim one weekend I browsed a list of educational career openings and stumbled onto a job description for an English teaching position at a large charter school in the northern part of the state. I was impressed by the fact that the curriculum emphasized the components of a classical liberal education. For whatever reason the job sounded appealing to me, and I'd been itching to get out of L.A., anyway.

They Skyped me from up there, and then we had three separate Zoom interviews, and a couple of months later I found myself behind the wheel of a twenty-six foot U-Haul, heading to my new home just south of the charming city of Eureka.

I arrived in the middle of August, about ten days before the start of classes. The sights and smells of Northern California, when I first stepped out of the van, brought a flood of unsummoned memories. For a brief moment I was a kid again, standing next to a little girl inside a dilapidated old cabin, playing house with each her, telling jokes, dreaming of our future together. Everything had seemed so real then. So exciting, so full of promise. But as always happens, life had gotten in the way.

The first thing I did when I got to Eureka, after meeting with my future employers and unpacking my boxes, was to seek out the local congregation of my church. This move to the northern part of the state wasn't just about the new job; it was the culmination of all the changes in myself that I'd been undertaking for the past several years – my weight loss, my healthier diet, my exercise, etc. A reboot of my life. And I'd known for some time that I'd gone on without God for far too long. So I showed up on Sunday, startling the members of my new congregation with my zeal and enthusiasm, making it clear that I was there to stay, and that I intended to be an active participant in every respect.

I also joined the local symphony orchestra, pulling my old cello out of its dusty case, playing classical pieces I hadn't touched in thirty years. It felt good, once the soreness in my fingertips had worn off.

I volunteered two evenings a week at the Women & Children's Emergency Center, part of the Eureka Rescue Mission, and I started putting in a full day, once a month on Saturdays, at the Sequoia Park Zoo. I mentored struggling students at a nearby elementary school, and I donated a substantial part of my income to tithes, offerings, and other charitable causes. I became busy, but in a good way. For once, my life had meaning.

THAT MOVE TO EUREKA, and everything along with it, happened almost two years ago now. It's been a great change for me. No regrets.

I've been sitting here typing these words on my laptop all afternoon. My wrists are getting stiff.

Setting the computer onto the bench next to me, I glance once more in the direction of my sweetheart. Then I lean back and close my eyes, allowing old memories to take over, surrendering myself to them as I've done so many times lately.

Right now I'm thinking about that day, two years ago, when I showed up at the school to meet with Jennifer, my newly assigned mentor. She'd insisted at the time that I switch classrooms with someone else, one of the other new teachers. I had absolutely zero notion at the time of the profound domino effect that her simple suggestion would have.

The recollection brings a smile to my face.

CHAPTER 2

JENNIFER

August 14.

It's truly an excellent school. Just under six hundred students altogether. I'm so glad to be here.

When the local school district decided to move all the seventh and eighth graders into a brand new junior high building ten years ago, several members of the board were in favor of simply demolishing the old building. Cynical locals accused them of trying to stifle competition from private schools, so they relented, joining the other three board members in a unanimous decision to sell the land with the building intact. Shortly after, a nonprofit which operated seven other charter schools throughout the state snatched it up, spent two years completely renovating and rewiring it, and opened, with much fanfare, the Eureka Academy of Science and Technology, or EAST.

In spite of the name (the acronym for which was a seeming misnomer since the new school, only blocks from the ocean, couldn't possibly have been located farther west), the curriculum objectives, which exceeded the state's minimum requirements, focused on those elements so often missing from modern education – the things which, taken together, had at one time been referred to as a classical liberal education.

Today, the school's mandate has hardly changed. Teachers are encouraged to improvise, be flexible, innovate, and do whatever is necessary to engage their students. But we're also not afraid to require extensive rote memorization, long reading assignments, and traditional classroom lectures, when appropriate.

It's this combination of old-style learning and college-worthy STEM instruction that has won EAST more than its share of awards over our eight-year history, and it's the reason that so many of the educators end up joining our faculty are above average. It's a great thing to be a part of, a model that's beginning to attract national attention, notwithstanding the ineptitude of our school board, comprised of appointed members with business backgrounds who think they know how to educate children better than we do.

I've just met our new teachers. Five of them. I've been assigned to mentor one of them, David, who'll be working in my department. He looks like he's in his mid-fifties, and I don't mind saying he's quite attractive for a man his age. There are only three other male teachers on our entire staff, so I view it as a highly positive thing that we've added a fourth. It's healthy for kids to not stereotype or pigeonhole job roles based only on sex. Gender diversity is a good thing.

I took David around and introduced him to Gloria, the principal, Beth, the HR director, and Ellen, one of the other new teachers. Then I gave him the grand tour, focusing on the school's highlights: the large auditorium with balcony seating; the Olympic-sized indoor swimming pool; the two-story library with real fireplaces and more than 15,000 volumes; the acoustic practice rooms for the band, orchestra and choir; the modern cafeteria with five separate ethnic food stations and a thirty-item salad bar.

I took him to his assigned classroom and showed him the inside, turning up my nose at the dim lighting and musty smell. I immediately recommended that he put in for an upstairs room in the B-Wing, on the other side of the building. The C-Wing side has always been drafty, out of the sunlight, and far from the faculty parking lot. It's a pain to get there, and all the other English classes are in the B-Wing anyway. I told him that the rooms on that side were much better than on this one, and that a B-Wing classroom should be his by rights, anyway, since he was going to be teaching eleventh-grade English. Further, I told him that Ellen, who'd be teaching geography, was replacing the teacher who'd been in the very room assigned to David, in the C-Wing.

He seemed to understand, and agree with, my suggestion. I told him he needed to go talk with Consuelo, the assistant principal, asap. Once the school year began it would be too late to make such a change. Time was of the essence.

CHAPTER 3

BOB

August 14.

I was appointed to the EAST board three years ago. Recently I became chairman. I'd like to think that my business background had more than a little bit to do with that.

I got my master's from the executive MBA program at Cal State, Stanislaus. I've filled a number of significant corporate roles, before and since – consulting, strategic planning, marketing, investment banking. Fortune 50 companies. Things of this nature.

Life's been good to me. Can't complain. Now it's my turn to give something back. Or what not.

My philosophy for Eureka has been, from the beginning, to bring a no-nonsense, business-based approach to the school board. Not to force it on everyone per se, but to persuade them of the superiority of American enterprise as it applies to actually getting things done. I want the teachers and administrators to run EAST more like a company, rather than a socialist utopia of feel-good platitudes, political correctness, racial sensitivity, and all that. Unacceptable.

Because it's all about the kids, after all. And what have you.

Anyway, we're gearing up for our mandatory kickoff meeting, before classes start, with all of the classified staff, including the new teachers, required to attend. Kind of a get-your-feet-wet kind of thing. Should be good. I plan to pull no punches. Let 'em have it from both barrels, so to speak. All that.

We'll see how it goes . . .

CHAPTER 4

CONSUELO

August 14.

I don't like men. Never have. Not that I'm a misanthrope by design; I just happen to prefer the company of women. Surely that's not such a hard thing to understand?

I applaud the #MeToo movement. I'm a staunch advocate of equal pay for equal work. And I detest the blatant sexism which is still pervasive in this patriarchal society of ours.

I'm comfortable working here, in this woman-dominated institution with its female principal. Mine is a relatively low-pressure job. I can allow Gloria to take on all of the social requirements of running a charter school while reserving for myself everything else: curriculum, finance, faculty, building organization, state certification, and on and on.

My master's degree in chemistry from UC Berkeley is, arguably, ill-used in this setting. But I don't care. I'm happy here. I get to spend most of the day behind my closed office door, wearing my intentionally frumpy clothes without even a single dab of makeup on my face, my hair always up in a bun, and my horn-rimmed bifocals perched on the end of my nose, attached to a dangling chain so I can pull the glasses down off my face and wear them like a necklace, whenever I want. I get to pore over numbers and spreadsheets and org charts and blueprints, all day long. Interruptions are relatively infrequent, and my recommendations are always taken seriously, because everyone here respects my intelligence. Perfect.

Gloria, as social as she is, gets far too uncomfortable whenever an upset parent wants to confront her about something. I, by contrast, welcome conflict, and enjoy helping people come to realize how their arguments are, so often, devoid of logic and reason. It's because of this that she's delegated all parental confrontations, as well as student discipline issues which have escalated beyond the classroom, to me.

I'm ever the tactful and professional one, of course. But I do admit to hating men, as I've said, and sometimes it's hard to not let this admittedly irrational bias of mine show. There's little in life I enjoy more than a good fight, especially when a protective, papa-bear father's involved. Particularly if he tries to intimidate or frighten me, or get in my face, or threaten legal action. I live for such clashes. Bring them on.

TODAY'S BEEN BUSY, so far. I worked on coordinating changes to the bus schedule, ordering some needed office equipment, and following up on a missing shipment of textbooks. I'm also in the middle of finalizing our new attendance procedures for the upcoming school year, composing a detailed reply to a facilities status update from the custodial crew, and preparing a press release to coincide with the first day of classes. I like to keep myself occupied. Something of a workaholic.

But this morning my cat killed, and then dragged into the garage, a beautiful brown-and-orange woodpecker. So I was already in something of a bad mood, for reasons other than the normal stress associated with the day's workload, when there was a knock on my office door.

"It's open," I called from my desk, fingers on my keyboard, halfway through a sentence. I heard the handle turn and assumed that someone had stepped inside. I didn't look up. Instead, I resumed my typing, not wanting to lose my thought, mid-sentence. Whoever it was would make her presence known, soon enough.

Indeed, only a few seconds passed before I heard someone clearing his throat. A man. Yay.

I looked up.

He was new. One of the recently-hired teachers, no doubt. I'd been out of town for a couple of the interviews, so I hadn't met this one yet.

I like to feel that I can be a bit intimidating, even when I'm sitting down. Especially with new employees. But this guy didn't outwardly show any concern. He was older, and obviously experienced. I couldn't help frowning. He hadn't said a single word yet, and already I disliked him.

"I'm David Mendoza," he began, flashing me a friendly smile which I did not return. "Your new English 11 teacher."

He waited for me to say something. I stared at him, hoping to make him squirm a bit. He stood there and stared back, patient, apparently not bothered by the silence between us.

"What can I do for you, David Mendoza?" I finally asked.

"I'd like to request that you switch my classroom from the C-Wing to the B-Wing. With the other English teachers. I want to be with my own group."

"Sorry," I said, returning to my typing. "Those rooms are already taken."

He didn't leave.

"Did you need something else?" I asked.

"Are all the classrooms in the B-Wing occupied by English teachers?" he asked.

I looked up at him again. He was evidently in his fifties, like me. It was equally apparent that his physical appearance mattered to him. He wore a manly Polo shirt and fashionable jeans, and I could smell his aftershave. I was sure he'd made more than his share of conquests among the other, weaker members of my gender, in his day. Presumptuous, no doubt. Apparently pushy. Entitled. Egotistical. Exactly the kind of man I despised.

"Mr. Mendoza," I began slowly, "your job here is to teach English, not to organize the layout of the school. The occupational makeup of the particular instructors assigned to the B-Wing of this campus is, therefore, not your concern. I assure you that, when the room assignments were made, every relevant factor was taken into consideration. Your assigned room is in the C-Wing. I have no intention of changing it. And as you can see, I'm in the middle of an important document, so if you have nothing else for me . . ."

Still he didn't leave. It was hard to detect, subtle, but I could sense a bit of anger rising within him. Good.

"My mentor, Jennifer Carson, said I should come and talk with you about it," he said.

"Did she? Well, now. Ms. Carson, like you, teaches English. The methodology behind the assigning of certain classrooms to certain teachers is therefore not any more relevant to her, than it is to you."

"I see."

"May I ask," I went on, "whether there's a reason for your desire to switch rooms this late in the process? Barely one week before classes begin? Is there something wrong with your classroom? Some custodial or maintenance need, of which I should be aware?"

"No," he said. "The room's fine. I was just hoping to be closer to my colleagues."

"And closer to the parking lot, no doubt," I said.

"I didn't say that."

"No, you didn't. And I'm certain that the proximity of your faculty parking space has nothing at all to do with your request."

I stared him in the eye. He finally shrugged.

"Ok," he said, turning to leave. "I tried."

He headed out the door.

I was almost disappointed. I'd been hoping that our little dispute might escalate. This David Mendoza seemed a worthy enough adversary.

He looked just a bit flustered, when he went away. Leaving open the possibility of future confrontations, which might prove to be splendid. Because in addition to my illogical prejudice against men, I also must own up to the grim yet unavoidable reality that I actually have very little respect for English teachers in general. Especially certain male English teachers, who seem to think that they're heaven's gift to women. Spare me.

I suppose I'll have to try to steer clear of the guy, moving forward. Gloria puts up with my quirks, but she'll be less than thrilled if I start to go out of my way to pick fights with her male staff.

This is looking like it's going to be a long year, I think.

Anyway. It's late in the afternoon now. Time for me to head to the pool and swim my laps.

I hope I'll be alone. Shouldn't be anyone else there, since school hasn't started yet. I hate it when other people are there, watching me swim. When I'm in the pool, there's nothing I crave more than solitude.

CHAPTER 5

ELLEN

August 14.

Pancakes. Again. But they keep eating 'em, so I keep cranking out more. LOL.

Thanks be to the heavens above for those big 'ol boxes of Great Value pancake mix. Gotta love Walmart. Great place to shop, IMHO. I really don't care what anyone else says about it. Haters gonna hate. Whatever.

Ok. I can do this. It's their weekend with their dad. He'll be picking them up 2nite. Just a few more hours. They'll be gone for like the whole weekend. Two glorious days. Woot.

It's not that I don't love the little stinkers, but sometimes a girl needs a break. This is one of those times.

I had to hurry to get them ready for day care. I hate it when we're late and they miss the stinkin' carpool. I was *not* going to let that happen this morning. So I was, like, focusing on the checklist all morning – lunches packed, hair combed, yesterday's shirts in the dirty clothes hamper, homework in backpacks, teeth brushed – *with* toothpaste, Chapstick on their lips. All set. Whew.

What am I going to do with all my time, 2moro? Easy question. Day spa treatment for the nails; Polish dog from Costco with a mountain of onions piled on top; *While You Were Sleeping* on Netflix; and a good Nicholas Sparks novel (even though I've read them all), before bed. Excellent.

BTW, I met with the other new teachers and the principal yesterday. The principal's nice. Her name's Gloria. I think I'm going to love this job. And this school.

One of the new teachers is, like, kind of hot. Even though he's, like, a gazillion years older than me. Whatever. I tried to make it *not* look like I was flirting, haha. *Tried.*

I'm in my new classroom now, setting things up. A USA map on this wall, a world globe on that table in the corner, some travel posters to make things exciting. This is fun. I put the chairs into a semicircle – I'm a big fan of group discussions, you know – and I can't stop thinking about the weekend.

So *bad.* My new job hasn't even started yet, and already I'm losing my focus. But education can be so *boring*, I hate to say. Seriously, though. Am I right, or am I right?

Gloria comes in and apologizes, seeing I'm in the middle of setting things up, and tells me she needs me to switch rooms. She's going to give David, the new English teacher, this room so he can be closer to his peers.

"Not a problem," I say, packing up my things to move to my room in C-Wing. "No worries." I want to make a good first impression. Gloria thanks me profusely and offers to help move my stuff. Everyone's so nice here.

Fifteen minutes later I'm setting things up in my new room. FWIW, it's on the first floor, rather than upstairs, which is fine with me. No stairs. Cool.

I'm thinking again about my weekend. Maybe I'll take a Sunday drive through the wine country – not Napa or Sonoma, but Andersen Valley, on the coast. A long way from here, but it might be just the thing. We'll see.

David is gracious in the room-swap. He pops his head inside the door, like, several times, asking if I need any help. He smiles as I giggle and make little jokes and stuff.

Can he tell, I wonder, that I'm a divorced mother, with two kids? Probably. But he's not wearing a wedding ring. Neither am I.

CHAPTER 6

DAVID

August 15.

It is better to dwell in a corner of a housetop, than with a brawling woman in a wide house.

Proverbs 21:9

I GOT my stuff loaded into my C-Wing classroom, determined not to allow yesterday's hostility from Consuelo to taint my good mood, nor my enthusiasm for this new job. Jennifer Carson stopped by as I was unpacking, asking why I hadn't moved to the room in the B-Wing, as she had recommended. I explained.

"Ah, of course," she said knowingly. "I should've thought of that. Should've warned you. Consuelo's a man-hater. But she's also one of my best friends." She held up her hand and said, "Stop unpacking. I'll be back in five minutes."

I sat down in one of the chairs, amused, and pulled out my cell phone to check my emails.

True to her word, she was back before I'd had time to get through them all.

"It's settled," she announced triumphantly. "Gloria agreed with me that this is not the right place for you. Come on, I'll help you bring your things."

My B-Wing classroom, though upstairs, was definitely better than the one I'd left. Roomier, with more natural light, and much closer to the parking lot.

Jennifer told me that Gloria had switched me with Ellen, the new geography teacher. She assured me that Ellen didn't mind. I made a point of going down there anyway, while Ellen was setting things up, to see if she truly wasn't disappointed.

"I'm the guy whose room they swapped out, with yours," I said.

"I should've known," she said with a smile, in the middle of taping the edge of a poster of Venice to the back wall.

"You gonna be ok down here? I don't want you to end up with a room you don't like."

"I *hate* this room," she said, still smiling mischievously. "You owe me big time."

I looked at her with surprise. She laughed.

"Kidding! This room actually works better for me. I like being on the ground floor. I'm glad we switched. Really."

I was relieved.

"Truth be told," I said, "they told me the other room – the one you moved out of – is newer. Better, somehow. I don't know about all that. I'm just glad to be closer to the other English teachers. When it comes down to it, now that I've seen both rooms, I'd say they're about the same, as far as that goes."

"I know, right?" Ellen said, going back to her desk to pick up another poster.

I left her to her tasks, returning to my own room to get it ready.

When I'd mostly finished setting up my own room about an hour later, the assistant principal, the one with the reading glasses that hung on a chain around her neck, walked past my open door, stopping to take a look inside. She stepped into the room and glared at me.

"What are you *doing*?" she demanded. Obviously no one had told her that Ellen and I had swapped rooms. She looked none too pleased about it.

I glanced around at the things I'd put on the walls, and at my arrangement of the chairs and other furniture in the room.

"I would think that would be obvious," I said. "I'm setting up my room."

"This is *not* your room. I thought I made that perfectly clear to you, yesterday."

It seemed like a silly thing to me, and I knew that Ellen was perfectly fine with the change in classrooms. This bellicose assistant principal seemed to be making a huge deal out of nothing. And she was fuming.

I could've humbled myself and asked for forgiveness, or tried to explain. I probably should've. But something about her belligerence brought out the fighter in me.

"This is indeed my room," I said, "and remembering how very busy you were yesterday afternoon, I'm sure you have other things to do that are much more important than to stand here and squabble with a nobody like me. And frankly, I have things I need to get done, too, so if you have nothing else to say to me, I'll bid you good day and get back to what I was doing."

"How dare you speak to me like that!" She was livid. She stepped further into the room. "Are you aware that I could have your position terminated?"

"Not my position. No. You're still going to need an English 11 teacher, even if you fire me specifically. Which wouldn't be the wisest thing to do, with school starting next week. And I will tell you that I've been courted by the teachers' union, which, I understand, requires that a very specific list of steps be followed, if you're going to terminate a teacher. Could take a while, as I understand it.

"So yes, I realize that it's within your power to begin the process of eliminating me. But I've also been around long enough to know that you have zero real intention of doing so. For one thing, Beth and Gloria would be very put out. For another, you don't have sufficient grounds. Not any grounds, as far as I'm concerned. So I'm calling your bluff. I *dare* you to terminate me, for being so audacious as to swap classrooms with Ellen, after Jennifer told me that Gloria instructed her specifically, to tell me to do that very thing.

"But whether you do or don't choose to take any further action on this issue, keep one thing in mind – I don't appreciate threats. Or bullying. This room in which you're standing is my assigned classroom. If you have a problem with that, you're free to take it up with the principal. Now stop wasting my time. And get out of my room."

CHAPTER 7

GLORIA

August 15.

Jennifer Carson pulled another one of her stunts today.

She came into my office and casually requested that I allow David and Ellen to switch rooms, assuring me that it would be completely fine with Ellen (it was). She conveniently omitted the fact that Consuelo was opposed to the move, even when I made a point of asking her how my assistant principal felt about it. I suggested to Jennifer that she take the matter up with Consuelo anyway, since Consuelo's the one in charge of such things, and it always seems to backfire for me when I second-guess her decisions or overstep my bounds. But Jennifer tactfully replied, with a twinkle in her eye, that discussing this particular issue with Consuelo might not be such a good idea, given Consuelo's history of openly discriminating against men. Our staff is almost entirely comprised of women, and I'd forgotten just how misanthropic my assistant principal can be. Jennifer and I shared a healthy giggle as we pondered the prospect of Consuelo confronting the new teacher over his room assignment.

Professional that she is, Consuelo is uncharacteristically raw when it comes to the opposite sex. More than once I've wondered whether it's just coincidence that so few men happen to work at this school. I've pushed that thought out of my mind, not wanting to dwell on it, letting it slide because I know Consuelo has her reasons. But I agreed with Jennifer that leaving Consuelo out of the particulars of this specific classroom switch might be for the best, especially if Ellen had no objections. And it did seem to make more sense, in terms of the layout of the school, given the locations of the other English classes. So I approved the change, and sent Jennifer on her way.

Tomorrow night's the school board meeting. Including some mandatory business training for the administrators and teaching staff, from Bob. They've set aside an entire hour for it. *Groan.*

I'm not a fan of Bob's approach. Not even a little bit. He's so . . . conservative. Always quick to shake my hand and tell me what a great job I'm doing, but deep inside, I know he can't stand me.

Everything he says comes across as totally insincere – his compliments, his suggestions, even his humor. Completely canned.

Not looking forward to tomorrow. Maybe I can call in sick? An hour of Bob's fluff. Heaven have mercy on me. Please allow me to be instantly crushed by a falling piano, or something. Seriously. Anything to spare me the agony of a grating hour with that man. Arrggghhhhh.

CHAPTER 8

JENNIFER

August 16.

Mandatory school board meeting. Classic Bob.

Here are some snippets which I took (verbatim) from somewhere in the middle of his "training," which consisted of nothing more than his lecturing us for almost sixty minutes while we fought to stay awake:

"Going forward, we're gonna be shifting the paradigm around here, ok? Moving it outside the box, running the needle up the flagpole to see if it sticks, all right? Because at the end of the day our bandwidth is limited. We've gotta keep this thing scalable. We're all team players here, right? We need to make sure the playing field is level. Looping everyone in, ok? Because a playing field that's not level is unacceptable. *Unacceptable*. Which means, I can't keep all the low-hanging fruit locked away in my silo, can I? That's not 360-degree thinking. I've got to circle the wagons back around, take this thing offline, tear down my silo, raise the bar, and all that. Team player, right?"

He was looking at us for some sort of response. At least, I think he was. My own eyes were mostly glued to the floor as I sat there, hoping against hope he wouldn't call on me. The other school board members seemed to have long since zoned out.

Bob continued to scan the audience for questions or comments. No one spoke up, so after a minute, he went on:

"We're gonna put our assets in the pipeline and leverage them, ok? Let's get granular on this thing, and what have you. No more drinking from a firehose. We're gonna peel back the onion. And I don't mind saying, I think this is an idea that really has legs. There's a synergistic effect, you know, that comes from showing the world we're willing to eat our own dog food. One plus one equals three. Because we've buttered our own bread; now we've gotta lay in it, if you take my meaning. Best of breed. Best practices. All that. It's the net-net of our boots-on-the-ground strategy. We've really gotta sharpen our pencils on this, if you get my drift.

"Granite, the optics have gotta look good. Milking the old cash cow, you know. Things of this nature. So, let's go ahead and put some lipstick on this pig. Raise it up the flagpole. Stick to our core competency. Become agents of change. Otherwise, what are we really doing here? Ready, fire, aim, right? Not gonna work. Unacceptable. What I'm giving you is the 30,000-foot view, you know, the 80-20 rule about what's actionable, what the deliverables are, all that, ok? Too many chiefs and not enough Indians in the kitchen, and what not. Something like that."

The breadth and depth of Bob's business knowledge is truly staggering. I'm sure none of us who were at the meeting would even know where or how to begin to respond to the steady stream of critical information he pumped into us tonight. A lifetime of vital experience from the thrilling world of American commerce, condensed into a brief, sixty-minute diatribe of clichés and mixed metaphors, solely for our personal edification and enlightenment.

If things hadn't been entirely clear prior to tonight's mandatory meeting, Bob did a bang-up job of sharing his vision with us. How could any of us possibly entertain any questions, or doubts, about the mandate of the board, after being so thoroughly "trained?"

In all seriousness, my evening was disastrously spent listening to the man spew for an hour while carefully avoiding any eye contact, and now I'm completely drained. Emotionally spent. Empty of everything but sarcasm and disdain.

Thanks for that, Bob.

CHAPTER 9

DAVID

August 22.

I said, Days should speak, and multitude of years should teach wisdom.

Job 32:7

SCHOOL STARTED. Everything went well, especially because I made a point of avoiding Consuelo, the assistant principal. Which was easy, because she was evidently avoiding me, as well. I always try to move quickly when I enter the school, walking past her office to get to the stairs, to head to my classroom. But her door's almost always shut, anyway, so I suppose it doesn't really matter.

Ellen doesn't seem to have minded taking the other room, at all. She's in her early thirties, and I think she's taken a liking to me. Not that I have the slightest interest in pursuing any kind of relationship with anyone. Been there, done that. Twice.

There was a ridiculous school board meeting the other night. At least an hour of mindless business-speak, presented with such earnest enthusiasm that it was difficult for me to sit still and not erupt into sardonic laughter. Somehow I made it through. But I fear I've inflicted irreparable injury to my tongue, after having bitten it so many times.

My students are similar in many ways to the ones I had in San Pedro. Kids are kids, I suppose. I particularly enjoy my fifth-hour class, A.P. English, because the students really seem to care about their grades and test scores, which makes teaching easy. For teens, they're a motivated, intellectual group. For the most part.

One of them, Jake Powell, is something of an obnoxious know-it-all, constantly whispering rude things to his buddy, Andrew. I had to tell the two of them to be quiet three separate times, on the first day of school.

Fadila sits in the back, wearing a headscarf. Her twin brother, Hasan, sits next to her. They're both fairly subdued. But I can tell, from my brief communications with each of them, that they're inordinately smart. Particularly Fadila. Borderline genius, I think. Has a huge vocabulary, from what I can tell. It's a shame that she hardly uses it.

Gerald's a lanky African American with size-fifteen Nikes and a look of perpetual boredom on his face. He surprised me when he offered more than one insightful answer, during the course of the lecture. I mentally caught myself, wondering whether my astonishment had been due to his sporty shoes and athletic build, or just the fact that he's a person of color. I hoped it was the former. Racism can creep up inside any of us, more often than not when we're completely unaware. Even – perhaps especially – when it's absolutely not welcome.

There are a handful of Hispanic kids, though when I spoke to them in Spanish none of them understood me, so I assume they must be later-generation Latinos, like me. And three southeast Asians sit together on the front row – second-generation Vietnamese, I think. There's also a native American girl named Carrie.

I'm enjoying the racial and intellectual diversity of the class, looking forward to some meaningful time together, excited to get to know each student on a personal level.

My first lesson was intended to impress upon everyone the importance of English. Not the language per se, but the class. We talked about what we would be learning together in the upcoming year: literature, grammar, vocabulary, logical fallacies, persuasive speech, the rudiments of good writing.

"In other words," blurted Jake without my calling on him, "pure fluff." He'd come from physics in his second hour, information systems in his third, and calculus in his fourth. Several members of the class glared at him and rolled their eyes. He didn't seem to notice. Apparently this wasn't the first time he'd openly challenged an English teacher.

"Whether it ends up being fluff," I said, "depends entirely on what you're willing to make of it." The students were watching the two of us expectantly, like passersby on a freeway, gazing at a recent accident at the side of the road.

"I've been speaking English," Jake said, "since I was two years old. I've taken enough English classes to last a lifetime. And then some. This is gonna be nothing but a waste of time. Everyone knows that. English. What a joke. If they'd just let us take the A.P. test without having to go through the pain of taking this loser of a class, there'd be no one sitting here in these seats right now. Such a waste of time."

Of course he was trying to goad me. Obviously he meant to engage me, to put me on the defensive. I shouldn't have let his comments get to me. But the inner fighter in me sometimes can't just blow things like this off. I took the bait.

"So Jake," I said, "if it were up to you, your ideal high school would have nothing but STEM classes?"

"Absolutely. Science and math are hard skills, Dude. English is soft. Touchy-feely. And all the good jobs are in science and math, anyway. And computers. Everything else is just feel-good fluff."

I turned to face the rest of the students.

"Jake seems to think that a high school graduate with nothing but math, computer and science skills will have everything he or she needs to do well in today's world. The four years of required high school English are therefore largely useless. Or am I misspeaking, Jake? I don't want to be putting words in your mouth."

Jake took a look around, frowning, ready to take me on.

"Dude, high school should take two years, not four. No fluff classes. Get everyone through earlier. Get us moved on to college. In job interviews the thing that matters is your technical knowledge. No one cares if you know how to read Shakespeare."

"Understood. Ok, let's establish a few givens, though: four years of high school English, if you have decent teachers and you actually do the work, will in fact accomplish *something*, will they not? You simply don't view such an accomplishment as particularly necessary, or beneficial. At least not when compared with what you'll get out of STEM classes. Agreed?"

"Sure," said Jake. "I mean, you're probably gonna try to make us read *The Scarlet Letter* this year. Or *The Great Gatsby*, or something. Maybe you'll teach us how to write a poem. Stuff like that. Big whoop."

"Ok. So, my question is, what is the *something* you stand to accomplish, it you take my class seriously? What are you going to gain?"

"I don't know. You tell *me*."

"Fine. I will. Six things: exposure to important literature, improved grammatical skills, a bigger vocabulary, the ability to recognize common logical fallacies, a toolkit for being more persuasive in your speech, and the ability to write well. Not a bad payoff, for an hour a day."

"Whatever," said Jake. "I'll never use any of it."

"But think about it," I persisted, "English is the language of *science*. A lot of good your physics is going to do when you're an engineer someday, if you can't explain yourself, or effectively put your ideas in writing."

"Nah. I already know how to speak, thank you very much. Learning a bunch of poems isn't going to improve the way I talk."

"Maybe not. But poetry isn't going to be our focus this year. What about logic? Reason? Do you think there's never going to be a time in your life when you're going to have to persuade someone to do something?"

"Maybe," he said, "but I already know how to do that."

"Do you?" I asked. "I wonder how persuasive your arguments have been, here, today, to the rest of this class, as they're sitting here listening to you? Should we ask them?"

"Go ahead," he said, not looking at anyone.

"No. I'm not going to put you on the spot. I actually think your concerns are legitimate. I *don't* want my class to be fluff. In fact, I want this to be the most important class you'll take, in your entire four years of high school. That's my goal."

"Hah!" he said.

"Hear me out," I said. At this point I was less interested in convincing him than I was in making my case to the rest of the class. They needed to know why they were there. Why this particular class should matter to them.

"English is the international language of business. Next to Mandarin Chinese and Spanish, it's the third-most widely spoken native language in the world. And think about this – more people around the globe study English – 1.5 billion of them – than any other language, by a factor of almost twenty-to-one.

"Any reasonable person, hearing that, would pause and ask why that is the case. Why would it be that so many more people study English, than any other language? What is it about this particular language that makes so many people want to learn it?"

"It's a conspiracy," Jake said. "From teachers like you." It was meant to be a joke, but no one really laughed. He didn't seem to mind.

"Very funny. But consider – English is the universal language of air traffic controllers. It's the official language of the Commonwealth of Nations, the International Monetary Fund, the World Bank, OPEC.

"And think about calculus, or geometry, or trig. Any math problem is only meaningful when it can be applied to real-word situations or conditions. We call them *story problems*. Every story problem has to be carefully worded, with precision and exactness. In English. Presidential debates; more than half of the world's websites; text messages to your friends; access to news and weather; user instructions; Hollywood movies; hip-hop music; emails; voter information. It's all English."

I looked at him before continuing.

"It stands to reason," I said, "that since such a large portion of your waking hours will be defined, enhanced, and controlled by your grasp of this ubiquitous and essential resource, and since virtually every other person you encounter in life will wield this same means either as a weapon to gain power over you or a subterfuge by which to handle or manipulate you, that whatever advantage you might gain through the process of adding to your existing skillset, will prove extremely beneficial.

"Without good English, your computer or math abilities aren't going to make much of a difference to anyone. You can create the most amazing pivot table in Excel; you can write a killer script to run on top of a massive MySQL database; maybe someday you'll be able to integrate the holographic principle of quantum gravity into the known laws of thermodynamics through your observations of black-hole event-horizons. But none of these things will matter, if you can't adequately transmit your ideas to other people. You might end up being the most brilliant scientist in the world, but if some other schmuck, with an intellect far inferior to your own, has a better grasp of the subtleties and nuances of our common tongue, your whole life will be spent watching that person excel while you get left behind, again and again.

"You want to get a good job? Take your STEM classes, by all means. But be the guy who *also* is able to communicate effectively. Be the well-rounded, well-read, educated person who inspires confidence in others. Who not only has great, original ideas, but who can translate those ideas into words that other people can understand. And appreciate. *That's* the person the world's employers are looking for. That's what English can do for you. That's what *this class* can do for you."

Jake rolled his eyes, but his desire to continue the debate seemed to have left him for the moment.

"We'll see," he said.

"Fair enough," I responded. "We'll see."

I turned and made my way back to the dry erase board, having the satisfaction of knowing I'd made my case. I could sense that the other students were on my side, ready to take from me whatever I could dish out to them, in the coming months.

Success.

CHAPTER 10

GLORIA

September 3.

Teacher development day. Eight hours of in-service meetings and employee training sessions. I've been looking forward to this all month.

The entire teaching staff, all 31 of them, met with me and the other administrators in the cafeteria, first thing in the morning. I'd had Abdullah set up the tables in a hexagonal formation, in advance, so we'd all be facing each other. There were water bottles and snacks at each place setting.

I'd purposely avoided microphones, podiums, or printed agendas. I'm a believer in equality within group discussions, and I feel that sometimes our very best work comes out of moderated brainstorming activities, rather than top-down lectures. So we all sat there in our makeshift circle of desks, looking at each other, ready to discuss the various aspects of our shared profession.

After covering a few not-so-urgent announcements, I decided to start the ball rolling by posing a broad yet vital question to the group, urging my staff to willingly contribute to a (hopefully) robust discussion, with the aim of eliciting some insightful responses: What can we do, individually and collectively, to take EAST to the next level?

Jennifer was the first to speak up.

"It's impossible to answer your question adequately," she said, "without first defining terms. What exactly is the 'next level'? What does it look like? I mean, do we all even agree on what that phrase means?"

"Good point," I said, nodding. I liked her response, but I wasn't going to let her leave it at that. "So, Jennifer, how would *you* define it?"

She nodded, as though she'd been expecting me to deflect her question back at her.

"Part of me," she said, "feels like it should have to do with reaching those kids who are hardest to reach. The ones who sit in the back, or struggle, or have unstable home environments. The bored ones, the distracted ones. The ADHD kids, the ones with discipline issues, the ones with mental health problems. Depression. Anxiety. Difficulty focusing. Who have a hard time making themselves feel like anything in life really matters. I think the 'next level' for us might be as simple as defining who exactly those students are, and finding better ways to reach them. Engage them. Make a difference for them."

Stu Sutton, my calculus instructor who has a heart of gold and is as soft as a puppy, chimed in.

"She's completely right," he said. "I totally second what Jennifer has said. I mean, I've got kids who sit on the front row, always raising their hands. They're the first ones to dive into a complex equation, right? They get, say, 80 percent of my attention, on any given day. It's not that I don't try to make myself available to the quiet ones, too. The ones who sit toward the back. But it's hard. Those kids in the front are so . . . I don't know, aggressive? Demanding? It's like a competition for my attention. And the louder kids, the more assertive ones, always seem to win."

"I have no problem with us defining 'the next level' for EAST as being better able to connect with our harder-to-reach students," chimed in Lexi, our health teacher. "I think you guys have nailed it."

"I agree," said Molly, a physical education instructor who's also the girls' volleyball coach.

"Me too," added Phoebe, who teaches biology.

Now, I know Consuelo well enough to know that she was soon going to burst, if she didn't take it upon herself to speak up and voice her opinion on all of this. Indeed, I was counting on it. Counting on her to interrupt the train of thought, just to keep us all on track. To curtail an over abundance of group-think.

She didn't disappoint.

"It's all fine and good," she began, and I noticed several of the teachers shifting to the backs of their chairs, apparently settling in for a long diatribe, "for us to talk about how to reach our unreachable kids. But it doesn't really mean anything if it can't be measured. How are we going to know when we've achieved our goal? How can we even set a goal in the first place, if we can't measure it?"

"Yeah, yeah, it's all about the *testing* for you," said Stu. "Just the numbers. We know. But what about the *people* part of the equation, huh? In the end, those numbers of yours are just cold, lifeless statistics. We're talking about real people here. With lives. They've got to matter to us."

"Of course," Consuelo said. "I'm well aware that we're discussing kids here, not just data points. I'm only saying that if we can't put quantifiable yardsticks in place, we're really just spitting in the wind. I don't deny that a bunch of touchy-feely platitudes might help us feel better about ourselves. I mean, we can all sit around and give each other group hugs and sing Kumbaya for the rest of the day. But until we define exactly what it is we want to achieve, and what success is going to look like when we get there, we're not really accomplishing anything. In short, we need empirical data. I would think that *you* of all people, Stu, given your subject matter, would understand that. At the end of a semester, you can't assign grades to your students based solely on how they feel about the subject matter, or whether it gives them some sort of sense of belonging or something, right? They actually have to *know* the material. Fairly black and white. Or am I wrong?"

I tried to hide my smile. Consuelo can be so transparent. She always has to make her voice heard on issues like this one. Even though everyone already knows her stance, it doesn't matter. She can't just sit back and bite her tongue. She has to speak out. Bless her heart; she's determined to keep us on the path of clearly-defined, statistically verifiable success, notwithstanding the frustrations of some of the best of our staff.

For what it's worth, our test scores are substantially higher than those of the public schools in the surrounding area, even though our student population, demographically, falls right in line with everyone else. So something here *is* working, without question. Our educational model? Our unique staff? Or is it Consuelo's constant insistence on teaching for tests (much to the chagrin of the teachers themselves)? It's probably a combination of these things. But whatever the reason, I'm glad we always do so well. If it ain't broke, I certainly have no intention of fixing it.

"So, Consuelo," asked Jennifer, looking directly at her, "how would *you* propose that we should define, and measure, our success in reaching those kids who are hardest to get to?"

"Why, Ms. Carson," Consuelo said with a smile of mock enthusiasm, "I'm *so* glad you asked." Jennifer smiled back at her.

The two of them have an understanding with each other. They *get* each other. They've been close friends for years, after all. I sometimes worry that the staff feels that Jennifer gets unfair treatment, given the close relationship between me, Consuelo, and herself. I've tried hard to make it not feel like the three of us belong to our own little clique, but it's not always easy. We just happen to fit together particularly well. I can't help it if two of my best friends in the world happen to work where I do. So I often find myself making an extra effort to avoid any appearance of favoritism.

For the most part, though, Consuelo doesn't seem at all worried about impeding any perception of bias. I guess she doesn't share my concern. It apparently makes no difference to her, one way or the other, if some of the teachers think she plays favorites.

"Allow me to elaborate on certain . . . suggestions, my dear Ms. Carson," she said, "if you will. For your personal enrichment, and edification, of course." She winked at her.

"Please," Jennifer said, smiling back. "Do continue. If you feel so inclined."

"Oh, but I do. I *do*."

It wasn't the first time the two of them had lapsed into their silly little game of faux formality during one of our meetings. It was nothing more than a cute diversion for them, harmless enough, but annoying to the rest of us. Just when I was thinking of saying something to end the sarcasm and pull us back into the discussion at hand, Consuelo turned to face everyone and propelled herself back into her analytical mode.

As she began to explain her ideas in detail, Stu settled back in his chair, frustrated. Jennifer's smile reverted to a poker face, though I'm pretty sure she already knew exactly what Consuelo was going to tell us. We'd heard it all before. More than once.

"Measuring things like this is actually fairly easy," Consuelo began. "It's all about isolating variables, and comparing predicted results against actual outcomes. So, for example, we set a timeframe – three months, let's say – and we identify, by name, the students we're targeting specifically. We're looking for causality here, so we use an existing assessment at the beginning of the trial period, to determine the current status. We then set a target, to gauge the expected improvement over time, and we re-assess, in two months, the same group, comparing actual results to expected ones. We can factor out other potentially impactful variables by comparing our micro dataset with any changes in the school's overall population, and we can maintain a control group, for consistency.

"I have, in fact, an econometrics model I've created. It's an Excel spreadsheet, you know, based on test results, by student. A trendline analysis. You know, linear regression. Just a line on a graph, determined by least-squares math, drawn through a scatterplot of datapoints. The stronger the beta coefficient in my model, the better the thing works as a predictor of future behavior. So that can be our starting point, ok?"

Some of the eyeballs in the room were turning glassy. She was losing her audience. But she sounded so authoritative, as always, that no one dared challenge her. No one, that is, until David Mendoza spoke up.

"So, is this model of yours a simple regression, or multivariate?" he asked. I couldn't help raising my eyebrows a bit, impressed. So he spoke her language, did he?

"Because," he went on, "we'll need to know, of course, how it controls for outliers. And we'll need to know if there's heteroscedasticity. You know – we'll have to create an overlay of the standardized residuals on top of your standardized predicted values, so we can verify randomness. Because if the data are in a cone shape, your homoscedasticity is compromised, of course. And you may have a problem with multicollinearity."

Consuelo was speechless. She stared at David, not knowing what to make of the new English teacher. The other people in the room seemed to have come back to life. What had been rapidly sinking into an indecipherable explanation of unknowable things only moments before, had suddenly become an interesting topic to everyone again. The new guy not only was fluent in the language of Consuelo's erudition; he was even willing to take her to task, in a way that none of the rest of us had ever been able to do.

She was a bit flustered. Obviously unused to being challenged in this way.

"Of course, Mr. Mendoza," she stammered. "We'll be sure to account for those possible discrepancies."

"Even so," David continued, "if we limit ourselves to nothing other than using your spreadsheet to tie improved test scores to this new initiative, we'll ultimately fail, of course. Even if the data shows substantial improvement."

"How so?" asked Consuelo. "I don't exactly follow."

"No," he said smugly, leaning back in his chair. "You don't." He smiled broadly, folding his arms over his chest, looking directly at her.

The room was quiet. No one had ever openly defied Consuelo's authority like this.

She'd been momentarily caught off-guard. But she was a fighter, through and through. She quickly rebounded, glaring at him as we all sat there waiting for him to continue.

He didn't.

"So . . . are you going to enlighten us on this?" she finally asked, looking at him without even a hint of a smile. "Or should we just move on?"

He still just sat there, saying nothing. Just looking at her. He slipped the fingers of each hand into the other, sliding them comfortably behind the back of his head, elbows pointing out. He leaned back in his chair and grinned.

Consuelo scowled at him.

"Aren't you going to say anything?"

He continued to maintain his silence, not looking away, the curious smile still on his face. Awkward. Uncomfortable.

Consuelo sighed loudly, shaking her head before proceeding.

"Ok," she said. "Fine. Whatever. So anyway, I propose that we begin by targeting . . ."

"We will *fail*," David interjected, loudly, jarringly, "on two fronts." His voice cut through Consuelo's words like a razor blade, and she stopped speaking, mid-sentence, her mouth dangling open. It appeared that he'd deliberately been waiting for her to resume speaking, seemingly for the sole purpose of being able to interrupt her once she'd started. There was an audible gasp in the room, from more than one participant.

"In the first place," he continued, "we'll be putting too much faith in the accuracy of the assessment itself. How reliable can it actually be? Any number of unforeseen variables will inevitably *not* be taken into account: How much sleep the kids got before taking the test? Their nutrition? How fresh in their minds the concepts are? Whether they crammed the night before? The luck factor? Potential distractions in their individual lives? Current national trends? Recent news stories? Possible discrepancies in the administration of the test itself? The weather, on the day they take it? Their emotional state? The randomness of the questions? The ability of the assessment to measure their long-term retention? The language and wording of the questions? Any cultural or ethnic discrepancies which might make it harder for one kid than another to understand what's being asked?"

I saw Consuelo roll her eyes and shake her head, but David continued undaunted.

"Besides all of that," he went on, "how are we going to choose to interpret the data, once we have the results? Should each question be weighted equally? If not, who's going to make a judgement as to which question should carry more weight than another? Should the examination be a multiple-choice test, or fill-in-the-blank, or essay questions, or all of the above? In short, how objective can we truly be in empirically assessing the real progress of these kids?"

"I'll be sure to use a professionally designed instrument, Mr. Mendoza," Consuelo said. "All of these considerations have been taken into account many times, by scores of educators in the past, on similar assessments. These people know what they're doing."

"They know what they're doing, yes," agreed David. "They're creating highly imperfect instruments, as effectively as they possibly can, with the best of intentions, hoping people like us will be wise enough to use the tools in the way they're intended to be used: with a big grain of salt. A major caveat. A significant qualification, through which the results must be interpreted. The overriding concern among many test creators is that school districts too often will simply take the results at face value, reading far more into them than was ever intended, or merited, by the data.

"But the second way in which we're going to fail," he said, before Consuelo had a chance to rebut, "is arguably even more important than the questionable validity of the test results themselves. The biggest problem we face in this whole process is not what we'll be testing, but what we *won't* be testing."

He paused, looking around him, into the eyes of his fellow instructors. Stu Sutton seemed particularly engaged, as did a number of others. Was this David Mendoza to be their new champion, after all? Were things finally going to change at the school? Was the balance of power being disrupted?

"Do continue, by all means," Consuelo said, barely masking the mockery in her voice, sighing loudly. "I'm sure we're all on pins and needles, waiting to hear what you have to say next."

David smiled grimly.

"Yes, well, you already know where I'm going with this," he said. "Standardized testing at best can only measure mastery of specific concepts. It rewards quick answers to superficial questions. It incentivizes all of us to repetitively drill our kids on only a very narrow curriculum using outdated methods, often ignoring the latest research, which might be too new to be on the exam. And standardized tests all have what's known as "measurement error," which means the same person, taking the same test on a different day, might get a significantly different result. It's something no test creator has ever been able to prevent.

"In computer-graded tests like the SAT or the ACT, the questions which almost everybody gets right or which everyone gets wrong, are removed, after the fact, leaving the final scores to be determined within the context of a smaller, less statistically reliable dataset. Composed of nothing more than just a few key questions for each section, in many cases. And multiple choice tests defy current cognitive theory, which is that kids learn not by processing separate bits of information independently, but through making larger contextual connections. All tests struggle to measure that ability; they tend toward examining only tiny packets of information, independent of each other, completely unlike the things we all encounter in real life.

"The increase over the past twenty years in so-called high-stakes testing, much of it the result of No Child Left Behind, has yielded exactly *nothing* in terms of classroom improvements, measurable or not. No difference at all. But it has definitely had an impact. Districts nationwide have scrambled to achieve certain test scores in order to avoid what's been derisively called AYP jail, as you all know. Meaning that until recently, underperforming schools not meeting so-called

Adequate Yearly Progress objectives could get put on probation and ultimately be run by local governments.

"To steer clear of this, we teachers were compelled to cater our teaching to whatever questions the standardized tests might contain, irrespective of the actual needs, or personalities, or characteristics of our classes. Some districts were caught in widespread cheating scandals. Others encouraged underachieving kids just to stay home on testing days. But the worst part was that all of the things that *should* be part of a child's education – creative thinking, imagination, whole-picture views, far-reaching rational thought, breadth of experience, depth of understanding, natural curiosity, the arts, music, foreign language expertise, cultural skills, even so-called street smarts – were stifled. Buried. Ignored. Sacrificial lambs in the all-important pursuit of higher test scores across a handful of narrow subject areas. All of which makes me think that a better name for that well-intentioned yet ill-suited law should've been *Every* Child Left Behind. Or No Child Gets Ahead."

There were a number of knowing smiles and nods around the room.

"Ok," Consuelo interjected. "So you're suggesting that EAST should do away with all testing. Is that it?" She sounded annoyed.

"Of course not," said David, looking steadily at her. "That would be completely impractical. And wrong. It's certainly not what I'm proposing here. Nor is it the topic of discussion."

"Not the topic of discussion?" she said, a bit bewildered. "After you just now went on and on about the many supposed evils of test taking?"

"If you're trying to make it seem," he replied, pointing a finger at her, "that I somehow endorse the bogus claim that all testing is inherently useless and that it should therefore be eliminated, so that you can then turn around and refute such an untenable position, you're committing one of the most classic of all logical fallacies – the straw man argument. Any kid, in any of my classes, could easily have recognized it."

Consuelo was floored. She prided herself on her own prowess with the rules of logic. To be publicly accused of such a fundamental lapse was more than offensive. Her face began to redden.

"I never proposed eliminating all testing," David went on. "Nor would I. To suggest that such a thing is my position and then to attack that view, is to create, and then seek to destroy, a straw man. An imposter, not representative of my intentions. My purpose thus far has actually been only to point out the inherent errors in relying exclusively, or too heavily, on so-called measurable assessments to determine whether we're meeting our goals. You yourself started this discussion by insisting that our ability to reach out to our most difficult students would only be meaningful if it was measurable, through comparative test scores. I'm pointing out the consequences of limiting ourselves solely to that approach."

"I see," said Consuelo. "Thank you *so* much for enlightening us on these things. What, may I ask, would you suggest we do, as an alternative?"

"Reasonable testing can and should be part of the process," David said. "But only part of it. And not the key part. We can get a better, more comprehensive view of the success of our initiative by combining other tools with test scores. Good classroom observations from teachers. Documentation of actual student work. Direct evaluation of real learning tasks through in-depth classroom discussion. Student learning records. Student inclusion in decisions over the content of their assessments. Work sampling and portfolios. Practitioner control, in which we teachers take responsibility for our own curricula."

"Lovely."

Consuelo sighed again, slumping toward the back of her chair, looking with dismay around the room at the nodding faces of those who seemed to be aligning themselves with David, convinced by his arguments. "We may as well do away with trying to quantify our results at all, then," she said. "That way, we'll be sure to hit our goal, no matter what. Whether what we're doing happens to make any real difference or not. Doesn't really matter anyway, right? As long as we feel good about our efforts. That's the important thing. Classroom observations, indeed. Hah. As if *that* could in any way help us move to the next level."

David seemed to sense that she was becoming increasingly defensive, and that the other people in the room were all turning against her. I could tell that he was beginning to worry that the discussion was spinning out of control.

"Please don't think," he said, more gently, "that anyone here is trying to blow you off . . ."

"Please don't think?" Consuelo interrupted, her voice raised almost to a shout. "Please don't *think*? Don't ever ask me, Mr. Mendoza, not to think. And don't you dare patronize me. I won't stand for it. You've apparently managed to persuade a number of teachers here that it's ok for their kids to underperform. The notion that mediocrity is acceptable here at the Eureka Academy. Congratulations. You've done nothing more than to tell these people exactly what they wanted to hear. To validate their resistance to any sort of empirical yardstick for determining continuous improvement. Not a tough sell, I would think. You've essentially been passing out candy to a group of babies, then acting pleased and surprised when they've stuffed it into their mouths."

Consuelo can go too far, sometimes. She can lose sight of when it's time to stop. This was one of those times.

"Let's move on," I interjected, taking a quick glance at her. "This conversation is quickly devolving, into unproductive territory."

"Our primary way of measuring success," David said, looking into the eyes of the staff, apparently ignoring what I'd just said, "should come from the teachers. Individual progress reports, based on collected observations and output over a period of time, for each of our targeted students. We can use these reports, rather than Consuelo's spreadsheet, as the basis for predicting expected outcomes. Then, when we administer tests after the fact, we can verify what we've already discovered. Rather than using nothing other than the assessments themselves to drive the process."

He turned and looked at Consuelo, who'd apparently given up, washing her hands of the entire discussion.

"Whatever," she said, acting like she was no longer interested. "Let's move on."

"I agree," I said, shuffling through my papers to turn to the next item on the agenda.

"Not yet," David said, in his gentle yet riveting manner. He wasn't ready for his ideas to be dismissed. "For one thing, it wasn't my intention to monopolize this discussion. For another, I don't think we've arrived at any sort of consensus. Or even an overall pattern by which to proceed. Your topic, Gloria, is highly relevant. Broad enough and important enough for us to discuss all day today, if necessary. The fact that a certain person in this room apparently lacks the emotional maturity to entertain the possibility of a difference of opinion, should in no way quell the discussion at hand. We need to keep talking about this."

"Just *who* do you think you are?" Consuelo demanded, pointing a finger toward his face. She was shouting now. The rest of us squirmed in our seats. "Seriously. Who do you think you are? You've been working here for what, less than a month? Who gave you the right to come waltzing in and upsetting the apple cart, anyway? Why do you seem so compelled to fix something which is already successful? You're just a teacher. A *teacher*. I've seen your resume. You don't have any background in administration. Why don't you leave the running of this school to the professionals, ok? Just focus on your students. Stick to your English curriculum. Don't try to change the world here, in your first month. We happen to know what we're doing, believe it or not. We have an outstanding academic record, one which I'd be proud to hold up against the achievements of any other school in the state, public or private. I'm sure our stellar record was the thing that attracted you to this school in the first place. We didn't hire you to come and reinvent the wheel for us. Why can't you just leave well enough alone?"

"Because I know what's going to happen next," David said. "I've seen this movie before. Too many times. Gloria was the one who initiated the discussion this morning, hoping to get some buy-in from the rest of us. We contributed. Had some healthy discussion. But you, Consuelo, decided you didn't like the direction things were taking. So you silently vowed to take the whole thing offline. I know how this works. You're going to let it rest for a bit. Maybe a few weeks. Then you'll resurrect your own ideas in some closed-door setting, where no one will be there to stand up to you. Next thing we know, some new policy or program will be imposed on us, top-down, irrespective of our previous input. And I have a problem with that.

"I couldn't care less about how Eureka Academy compares with other schools. Education in America is, in many respects, a joke. The only comparison that really matters to me is how we're actually doing, versus how we *could* be doing. Or *should* be doing. Our own potential. What we can achieve, as a stand-alone institution, with zero regard as to how any other schools might be performing. No benchmarking, other than looking at our own history, and our room for improvement with respect to it."

He turned to look at me.

"The fact that you, Gloria, began this meeting by asking us to discuss how we can take this organization to the next level, indicates that you feel that there's value in engaging us, your teaching staff, in coming up with some answers. Which would suggest that, at least in your mind, there's room for improvement. That the existing paradigms and processes at EAST might be inadequate, moving forward. If you actually meant it when you said you wanted us to contribute to the conversation, then that's what we should be doing, right now. Rather than moving on. Especially if our only reason to do so is to avoid the potential for somebody's emotional tantrum."

He turned from me to Consuelo, just as she was rising from her seat, beet red.

"I don't have time for this," she said. "Why don't you all just go ahead and have your little 'discussion,' ok? I've got more important things to do. And apparently, my input isn't needed here, anyway. Or valued. So if you need me, you know where to find me."

She grabbed up her stack of papers and headed for the door.

"Consuelo," I called after her as she was leaving. She didn't acknowledge me. "*Consuelo.*"

She left the room.

David, neither gloating nor showing any sign of remorse, simply gave me a blank stare, as though Consuelo's behavior hadn't surprised him in the least.

"Shall we continue?" he asked.

CHAPTER 11

DAVID

October 1.

Let them be confounded and consumed that are adversaries to my soul; let them be covered with reproach and dishonour that seek my hurt.

Psalm 71:13

I NEVER GO to shopping malls. Ever. Haven't been inside one in ten years. Probably longer.

So it was on a total fluke that I found myself emerging from an aisle in the Walmart on Broadway, to head into the enclosed hallway inside the Bayshore Mall this evening. In a completely uncharacteristic way, I wandered aimlessly for a good twenty minutes, strolling casually past the storefronts, more interested in observing my fellow shoppers than the wares which were being offered for sale.

It was all a bit depressing, truth be told. Bayshore is, like any other American mall, dying a slow death, with only half of its spaces occupied. The number of shoppers was underwhelming, and just outside, along the north wall, a cluster of drug addicts crouched together, staring at nothing, trying to keep themselves warm. Old Town Eureka isn't what it could be, given its population of homeless people who roam the streets, with the boarded-up buildings and the empty lots along the waterfront. Kind of a shame, if you ask me.

The enticing aroma of freshly baked cinnamon rolls brought me back into the moment, and I instinctively redirected my steps toward the food court area. I bought myself a roll, sitting down at an empty table. The little niche was popular; most of the tables were already occupied.

I habitually pulled out my cell phone to start checking the news as I bit into the pastry. It was to die for. I allowed myself to slip into a déjà vu moment, picturing myself sitting in the old cabin as an eleven-year-old kid, eating my homemade cinnamon roll after polishing off my chips and cold bean dip.

The sound of someone laughing at the table next to mine in the mall, pulled me out of my daydream. I turned and saw three of my co-workers sitting there, giggling over some joke one of them had told – Jennifer, Consuelo, and Ellen. I smiled and waved. Ellen waved back, her eyes as flirtatious as ever. Jennifer nodded and smiled, as well. But Consuelo, having taken one look at me, turned back to her friends immediately, completely ignoring my existence.

I sighed. What to do now? It was a bit awkward, sitting there next to these fellow employees of mine. Should I stay at my table, alone? Would they think it was rude if I didn't join them? I wasn't in the mood for social interaction, but I also didn't want to come across as standoffish. Without further internal deliberation, I grabbed my tray and stood up, heading to the empty chair at their table.

"Mind if I join you?" I asked, sitting down before any of them could answer. They were looking at each other and not at me, caught up in another unspoken joke. Jennifer and Ellen looked like they were about to burst out laughing again. Consuelo, also in on the joke, was smiling, still refusing to make eye contact with me. I took another bite of my roll.

"Early Christmas shopping?" Jennifer asked, turning to me, trying to make conversation. Each of the women at the table had bags at her feet, on the floor. I had nothing. Nevertheless, I nodded my head.

"Jennifer," Ellen said, "that was a bit presumptuous of you, ok? I mean, maybe he's like, Jewish, you know? Like Hanukah, or something. Or maybe he's, like, one of those Kwanza dudes. And anyway, we're still a whole month away from Halloween, right? I mean, I'm just saying."

I smiled at the clumsy effort to be politically correct.

"Regardless," Jennifer said, "You can't deny that I guessed it right." She looked at me. "You *are* here to do some Christmas shopping, are you not?"

Again, I nodded.

"You must've just barely gotten here, then," she said. "You haven't bought anything yet."

"Not yet," I said absently.

"So tell us who you're shopping for," Ellen chimed in, with enthusiasm. "We can help you figure out what to get. We know *all* the sales." She smiled at me. "Seriously. How many people? What ages? Male or female? Stuff like that."

I paused for a moment, appreciating the not-so-subtle attempt to pump me for information.

"Actually," I said, "I wasn't really looking for anyone in particular. Just kind of strolling around, checking things out. Seeing what there is to see. You know."

"Oh," she said. "Well, you're welcome to join us, if you want to. We were just taking a bit of a break here, for a minute. We've barely gotten started, actually. Lots more to go. Totally."

My eye caught Consuelo jabbing at Ellen from beneath the table, openly frowning. Ellen turned and flashed a surprised look at her, Ellen's lips silently mouthing the word, "*what?*"

Consuelo cleared her throat, barely rolling her eyes. She sighed, turning to me.

"I'm sure the *last* thing a guy like him wants to do is hang out with a bunch of lowlifes like us," she said, loud enough for all of us to hear. "He probably cringed when he noticed we were sitting here in the first place. Came and sat at our table out of obligation. Politeness. No doubt he would've preferred for us not to have noticed him at all. So he could enjoy that big cinnamon roll all by himself. *Alone.*"

She was looking directly at me, now. Her face showed not even the hint of a smile.

"I beg your pardon," I said. "I didn't mean to intrude." I grabbed my tray, ready to return to my table. "Just trying to be . . . neighborly, I guess." I slid my chair backward.

"Wait," Jennifer said, laying a hand on my arm before I could get on my feet. "She wasn't asking you to leave. You're our *teammate*, after all. Besides, this all-girl party of ours is wanting, I think, for a bit of masculine company. Please don't go."

"Yes," said Consuelo, "*don't* go. You've graced us all with your presence. It just wouldn't do, at this point, for you to withdraw. One or more of us might be *devastated*, truth be told. We couldn't have *that*, now, could we?"

She looked at Ellen, shaking her head. Ellen turned three shades of red, looking away.

"However, ladies," Consuelo went on, "we'll need to modify our plans somewhat, to accommodate Mr. Mendoza's whims, I'm sure." She glanced at me. "So, what's it gonna be? Where would you recommend that we go first? The sporting goods section of Walmart, eh? Hunting? Fishing? Knives and guns? Or maybe we should all of us just go ahead and march straight to the women's lingerie area, hmm? I mean, why waste our time? I'm sure Ellen will be able to find any number of things on her list in that particular part of the store."

"Consuelo!" Jennifer said, trying too hard to make herself look scandalized, covering her mouth like she was about to cough, making an effort to keep from bursting out laughing. Consuelo saw her, and kept going. She was on a roll.

"Speaking of lingerie," she said, looking at me, "I don't suppose *you* have any specific needs in that department? I mean, you've made it clear that you don't intend to tell us *who* you're shopping for, let alone the gender, leaving us to our own resources to determine your true purpose. A little voice inside my head is telling me that perhaps you're in the market, not for a negligee or a slip for, say, that 'special someone,' but rather for such an article of intimate attire for your own, personal use. Or am I completely off the mark?"

I opened my mouth to respond, but before I could get a word in edgewise, she was spewing again.

"You obviously have nothing but disdain for societal norms and standards, as evidenced by your having taken advantage of a younger peer's goodwill by blatantly stealing her classroom from under her nose, for no other reason than that you stood to personally benefit by having a closer parking spot. You have no apparent regard for rules, assignments, organizational structure, or propriety whatsoever. That, coupled with the fact that you display an irrepressible willingness to pursue your own selfish ends, irrespective of whatever conflicts might result from your actions, with a blind eye toward any negative impact your choices might have on the organization as a whole, or on individual participants within it."

"Not true," I said. "Actually, I . . ."

"And you have no sense of *decorum*," she cut in, not ready for me to interrupt, "as you proved in that in-service meeting a few weeks ago, in which you insisted on foisting your own viewpoint onto everyone else, your newness here notwithstanding. This in spite of the fact that your job position in no way qualifies you to make organization-level decisions in anyone's behalf, at all. Your experience, better expressed as the lack thereof, contains nothing which would merit your shameless self-approbation in terms of your attempt to alter the school's strategic direction, insisting that we laboriously consider actually throwing out our highly successful model, with its proven track record, in favor of your own touchy-feely platitudes of nonsensical gibberish."

"That's not correct," I said. But that was all I said. There was no chance for me to say anything more. She was still going.

"Is it any wonder, then," she said, "that I should consider it quite in alignment with your character, or at least what I know of it, for me to suppose that you very well might be just the type of person who shuns societal norms and virtues, pursuing instead those things, prurient or otherwise, which might serve only to gratify your personal whims, stoking your already lofty ego? I therefore conclude that a direct trip to the lingerie department might be just the thing, not so much for us, but for *you*."

"Are you done?" I asked, amazed that I might *finally* be allowed to squeeze in a few words of my own. She nodded, still not smiling. Her two friends were already getting up from the table, ready to move on. She got up and stood with them.

I opened my mouth, not knowing where to even begin.

Jennifer and Ellen had already begun to walk away. Consuelo continued to stand there, looking at me.

"Coming?" she asked.

"I . . . don't think so," I said.

Without another word she simply turned and walked away.

CHAPTER 12

GLORIA

October 17.

I love this time of year. My husband and I took a trip inland, to see the gorgeous fall colors.

The school year's been going well. Our new hires are working out fine. If there were one thing I would change, it would be the assessment tool we emailed to the staff last week. Not that I don't consider it a useful way of gauging how we're doing and where we can improve. I'm certainly in favor of that kind of thing. But at the end of the survey the teachers were invited to rate us, the administrators. Which would've been fine if it had all been kept anonymous, as it was supposed to be. Consuelo, consummate professional that she is, can be trusted to keep everything completely confidential.

What was unexpected was that David, the new English 11 teacher, left a particularly harsh review, even taking the time to add several paragraphs at the end, in the "additional comments" section, detailing everything he thinks is wrong with my assistant principal. I know he's had several run-ins with her, and I guess he chose to use this online assessment survey to vent his frustrations.

While I'm open to feedback for the sake of continuous improvement, I really wasn't looking for specific criticism of Consuelo. I'm well aware of her quirks.

Truth be told, not only is she my best friend; she's also the single most valuable employee on my staff, and I would neither replace her nor critique her for anything in the world. Much of the success behind this school is due to her efforts, as both she and I are well aware. She has no desire to have my job, and I will be forever grateful that she's willing to take on every undesirable or unsavory task that would otherwise fall to me. And she does it without complaining, or making threats. It would be impossible to get on without her.

The problem came from the fact that she was the one who administered the survey, as well as the one who gathered and analyzed the results. When she encountered the scathingly critical input from David, it was immediately clear to her who'd left it, anonymity notwithstanding. The words were direct and specific, almost as though he'd wanted her to read what he'd written, and to know it had come from him.

He's become hugely popular with his students, one of several teachers whom I consider superstars among our faculty. I have no regrets over hiring him at all, and I think he'll only grow more valuable to us over the coming years. There's no call for me to reprimand him for being honest about his dealings with Consuelo, and I certainly wouldn't want to discourage him or jeopardize his enthusiasm to continue to work here.

Which means that two of my most valuable employees are at loggerheads with each other, and I can't really see a clear way to bridge the divide or otherwise bring them together. It's unfortunate, but for the time being, I think I'm going to have to advise each of them to steer clear of the other. Keeping them apart will probably be more helpful than hurtful, at least for now.

CHAPTER 13

DAVID

October 19.

Let all bitterness, and wrath, and anger, and clamour, and evil speaking, be put away from you, with all malice:

Ephesians 4:31

A BIT OF A MELANCHOLY DAY. I observed my traditional moment of silence this morning for the dead rat of my childhood, Pinqui.

I have to admit that I've been having second thoughts about the responses I left in an online survey I filled out last week. I gave the school high marks and rated all the administrators equally highly, with the exception of Consuelo, the assistant principal, who is, by all indications, a poor fit for her current position and in some ways more harmful than helpful.

I wasn't in the greatest mood when I took the survey, and I wrote some things at the end of it which, while honest, were neither tactful nor kind. I supposed she deserved it, and it's inevitable that she'll figure out that the words came from me. Which doesn't frighten me in the slightest – people like her definitely stand to benefit from a good dose of humility, every now and again – but my words were intentionally biting, and didn't reflect on me the way I like to think of myself. It wasn't my proudest moment. If I had it to do over, I think I'd tone it down a lot. Maybe I wouldn't do it at all.

What's done is done, though. Water under the bridge. She seems to have extremely thick skin, so the things I wrote will probably have little or no impact, anyway. Water on a duck's back. And I really don't think she gives a hoot, one way or the other, what my opinion is. So there's that.

I suppose I'll need to get some candy at the store this week, in case any trick-or-treaters come by on Halloween. One more item on my to-do list.

CHAPTER 14

BOB

October 28.

I'm very much in favor of internal surveys. Continuous improvement, and all that.

But the one I received this afternoon isn't sitting right with me. Someone took our assistant principal to task, looks like. Which, to me, is unacceptable.

Granite, she's not good with people, I'll give you that. Granite, she's a bit of a shrew, or an old spinster type, if you ask me. But I'm a team player, and I'll go to bat for her to hit one out of the park, because she can open my silo any day of the week, and leverage the assets I've got in there. But the playing field's gotta be level. The playing field's gotta be level. Otherwise, no dice.

The surveys were anonymous, so I don't know who the jerk was who decided to take a potshot at Consuelo, but it's exactly the kind of thing that's got to stop around here, if we're ever gonna shift our paradigm to a new flagpole. And things of this nature. So I'll be keeping my eyes open from now on, for clues, or what not. I wanna know who wrote this stuff about her, and what have you. Unacceptable.

Our attitude determines our altitude. And all that.

CHAPTER 15

CONSUELO

November 1.

I was sorely tempted, as I sat there across the desk from Hasan, to find a way to leverage the anonymous complaint that some spineless Islamophobe had lodged against him, into some sort of aggressive indictment against his English teacher, whose horrendously offensive diatribe against me in last week's administrative assessment tool was so obtrusive as to render me utterly unable to focus on the plight of the poor boy in front of me.

I looked at the kid, struggling to allow the words he'd just spoken to register, trying to push out of my mind the ludicrous personal attack against me in the form of a couple of spiteful paragraphs at the end of the survey from none other than Mr. David Mendoza, English teacher extraordinaire.

There is, of course, a thorough school safety plan in place, and any time a threat is suspected, real or otherwise, my duty is to perform an exhaustive investigation, documenting everything. There have been times when this level of diligence has seemed to be both fitting and appropriate. This was not one of them.

"Hasan, I'm sorry," I said, "but I need you to repeat what you just told me."

"I said I've never brought any kind of weapon to school," he said. "You can check my backpack. Just books."

"I believe you," I said. "No need to check. But I *am* required to ask you a few questions. Just like we've done before. Because it's policy. I have to follow the procedure, as you know."

"Go ahead," he said, not smiling.

I monotonously read through a list of questions: Have you ever visited a website or Facebook page from a known terrorist organization? Do you feel alienated from your classmates? Do you have a good relationship with your parents? Do you own, or have you ever owned, a firearm? His answers were terse, somber, mostly given in one word.

I felt bad for him. The kid was no fool. He knew exactly why I'd called him in, no matter how much I tried to downplay it. Someone had thought that somehow, simply because of his ethnic or religious background, he posed a threat to the safety of the other students.

At the end of our brief interview, he got up to leave.

"Wait," I said, rising from my desk. I put an arm on his shoulder.

"You have as much right to be here as any other kid in this school," I said. "I want to apologize, on behalf of the ignorance of people who jump to conclusions without a speck of evidence, simply because of their own deeply-held biases. I wish it weren't true, Hasan, but racism is alive and well in America. I hope you won't let it get to you too much."

He managed a tiny smile and assured me that he wouldn't.

I've already mentioned that I don't like men, but Hasan is an exception. Nice kid. Quiet. Takes care of his twin sister. He doesn't smile much, and it's often hard to know what he's thinking, but my gut tells me he's a good boy at heart. In that respect he takes after his father, Abdullah, the head custodian of the school. I suppose Abdullah deserves some credit for raising a couple of solid, decent kids.

Speaking of which, I have to add that as much as I'd love for David Mendoza to make some tragic misstep in his job which might justify my roasting him alive at the stake, I pride myself on being fair, and I have to give credit where credit's due. The man actually (amazingly enough) seems to have instilled a new degree of sensitivity among the juniors and seniors with respect to Hasan and his sister, who've been targeted more than once over the past several years.

This is not to imply, however, that the guy isn't also a complete jerk, whose very existence confirms every reason I've ever entertained to support my loathing for the opposite sex. I can't believe he wrote those things about me. I'm not worried about repercussions from Gloria; I've already shared his tirade with her. She adores me; I know she'd never even consider reprimanding me, much less letting me go. We've been best friends since grade school, after all.

But David Mendoza's another thing entirely. With those repugnant survey remarks, he's catapulted himself to the top of my list. Public enemy number one. My arch-nemesis. He'll think twice about picking a fight with me, before the semester's over. I'm not about to blow this off. He'd better watch his step, because I'll be right there behind him, waiting for him to fall.

Ok, enough with the clichés already. I'm starting to sound like a bad movie, haha.

It's been a long day. In an hour I'll be swimming laps. All of this will be far behind me. Can't wait.

CHAPTER 16

FADILA

November 1.

We missed the bus, because Hasan had to meet with the assistant principal. Again.

Someone complained about us again. No doubt about it. Like we're not Americans or something, because of our names, and the color of our skin. Like my brother's going to blow up the school or something. Whatever.

Now we have to sit here and wait, outside the janitorial closet, for Dad to finish his job and punch out on the timeclock. Life isn't fair.

Jake Powell was teasing me again this morning, about my hijab. He kept asking me why I have to wear it. Kept daring me to take it off. I hate, hate, *hate* that boy, when he acts that way. He was going on about the separation of church and state, how the school couldn't legally display the Ten Commandments or a cross or anything, so why did I get to keep wearing my headscarf? *So* annoying. It's a good thing Hasan wasn't there at the time, or Jake might be missing a few teeth. Then we'd have to go to the assistant principal's office, *again*. Ugh.

Ok, heads up: the next thing I'm gonna put down here is top, top, *top* secret. Whoever reads it, you'd better not tell anyone. *Anyone.* Seriously.

I'm starting to experience . . . *unnatural* feelings. For my English teacher. Mr. Mendoza. He's, like, three times my age at least, but there's no denying he's hot. At least, for an old guy. Today I sat there in the back, looking at him as he taught us, and I kept wondering what he feels about me. I'll be eighteen next year. He could legally be with me then, if he wanted to.

What am I *talking about*? Running off at the mouth, again. This is *so* crazy.

But he's *nice*. There's no one – not a single soul – who's my age, who's even remotely like him. No one at all.

Ok, enough about that. But more about Mendoza.

Jake Powell tried to mix it up with the guy again today. The subject was gun control, this time. What a joke. Every argument Jake presented was shown to be a logical fallacy. Very instructive to us, but Jake was pretty upset, by the end of class. Way to go, Mendoza! Humiliate the little punk!

I've been worried about Hasan. He's too much like Dad. Too impetuous. Emotionally unstable. Angry. The whole time Jake and Mendoza were going at it on gun control, my brother just sat there frowning, saying nothing. Brooding. Not good.

CHAPTER 17

JENNIFER

November 17.

Getting myself mentally geared up for Thanksgiving. Can't believe it's next week!

I'm so glad I talked to Gloria about switching David Mendoza's classroom in August. He's such a good influence; everybody loves him. It's been great to have him in our hall, with the rest of the department. I think his students really respect him. The rest of us are all female; it's nice to have a bit more gender balance.

There was, however, an unfortunate encounter in the lunchroom today. I usually eat in the faculty lounge, but David has made a point of sitting and eating every day with his students, in the cafeteria.

I happened to be there with Gloria, at the time. We were on a mission to grab some cleaning supplies for the teacher's lounge bathroom, which had run out of toilet paper. We'd been making our way toward the back of the room when I saw that Jake Powell was pestering the little Syrian girl, Fadila, about her headscarf, in front of everyone. Completely inappropriate. I paused and brought the incident to Gloria's attention.

Fadila had sprung up from her table. Her cheeks were flushed, and there were tears in her eyes. Her brother wasn't around. Before Gloria or I could do anything, I saw David get to his feet as well, moving over to where Jake and Fadila were standing. Jake was yelling something, taunting her, demeaning her. Then I saw his hand go for the hijab, like he was going to pull it off. He never made it.

David Mendoza's hand shot out so fast I almost missed it. He took Jake's hand and wrist in something that looked like a Judo hold, and all at once Jake was down on his knees, his arm twisted behind him, with David standing there over him, holding him down. David said something to Fadila, who straightened her hijab and ducked her head down, rushing out of the lunchroom. She met Hasan in the doorway; he must've been using the men's room or something. He took one look at Jake, still on his knees, and frowned before whisking his sister off, down the hallway.

When David finally released Jake, I could see that the kid was spitting mad, yelling and cursing, making rude gestures. David took it all in stride; he'd won this round, and everyone in the lunchroom had seen what had happened. He headed back for his seat at the table. Then, out of the blue, Jake walked up to him and swung a fist at his face.

David's reaction was too quick to have been anything other than pure instinct. He dodged the punch, stepped in closer to Jake, elbowed him savagely in the ribs, smacked him in the face with the back of his fist, and pulled him roughly to the ground, all in one deft, sweeping movement. It literally took less than a single second. I felt like I was watching a karate movie.

Jake was done. All desire to fight had left him. He lay there on the cafeteria floor, breathing heavily, wiping his bleeding nose.

Suddenly all of the kids were talking at once. All eyes were on Mr. Mendoza, who had dropped to one knee and was cradling Jake's head gently in his hand, turning him from side to side, checking to make sure there were no broken bones, looking into his eyes for any sign of a concussion.

Dan, the school security officer came rushing into the room, hand on his holster snap, demanding to know what had happened and whether anyone had bothered to call 9-1-1. Gloria was already heading over to the scene of the incident. I followed her.

David looked up from where he was wiping the blood from Jake's nose with a napkin. I thought he'd be apologetic. He wasn't.

"I couldn't let him pull the hijab off," he said simply, to Gloria. "Wouldn't have been right."

"There'll be an internal investigation," Gloria said. "Both you and Jake will have a mandatory, three-day suspension. We'll have a meeting, after that, to discuss this. But I want you to know that I was here, with Jennifer. We saw the whole thing. All I can say is, the kid had it coming to him. I'm glad you did it."

The room grew kind of quiet after that, and I turned and saw the reason why. Abdullah, the janitor, was walking toward us, a wide broom in one hand. Everyone was watching as he approached Jake, who was now sitting up, still on the floor.

When Abdullah reached him, eyes burning with hate, he spit on him. Right into his face. No one said a word. Jake wiped the spit with the back of his sleeve. Abdullah said nothing. He turned and walked out.

No one, not even Dan, made a move to stop him.

CHAPTER 18

GLORIA

November 18.

It's been cloudy and overcast for days now. A cold, light rain keeps drizzling, on and off.

We held our mandatory meeting in my office this morning, with David Mendoza, regarding his use of violence against a student. Beth was there, representing the H.R. department. Consuelo ran the meeting.

There were two separate surveillance video feeds which had captured the incident. We began the meeting by watching each of them. David sat comfortably in his chair, calm and self-assured, declining to offer any words to defend his position, suggesting that the video footage spoke for itself. There was some discussion as to whether the force he'd used was excessive. Whether it exceeded the bounds of self-defense.

Consuelo sounded cold and clinical throughout. I was surprised to see how tense she was as she cited endless paragraphs of school policy, speaking in overly formal tones, referring to David as "the accused" and Jake as "the victim." Never once did she look David in the eye.

When the meeting had been going on for more than an hour and I could see that she was about to launch into another lengthy set of obscure paragraphs of legalese, I stopped her.

"Can we cut this short?" I asked. "I'm sure we all have things we need to get back to. I appreciate your thoroughness with this, but I think at this point we're only beating a dead horse."

"I second that," Beth said. "We're familiar with school policy. We know the facts of this case. I don't understand why you keep insisting that we pore over this minutiae, in such painstaking detail. It's almost as though you have a personal vendetta against Mr. Mendoza. It's like you're using this time to indirectly air your grievances. The truth is that all that's left for us to do at this point is to make a decision, and then move on. Let's stop dragging the thing out."

Consuelo looked at each of us and shrugged.

"Please know," she said, "that my conduct in this case has nothing to do with my personal feelings toward any of the individuals involved in it. You two know me well enough to know that I always follow a strict policy of data-driven decision making. I'm simply trying to make sure that the three of us, who will be choosing the direction we'll need to follow, are armed with all the facts. Our decision today should be based on *data*. Not on feelings, or opinions."

"Of course," I said. "No one's questioning that."

"Not true," David said. "I'm questioning that."

We turned and looked at him in surprise. It was the first time he'd really made any comment about the incident, or the case that had been laid out before him by Consuelo.

"Data, by itself, is incapable of making, or even driving, decisions," he said. "It's really nothing more than a cluster of plot points, on a graph. On its face, it has no inherent meaning. It's just a bunch of numbers. It can't make your decisions for you. It can't even color one choice as more compelling, or evident, or striking, than another one, until you first apply your own assessment to it."

I turned to Consuelo, who rolled her eyes.

"There's no such thing as data-driven analysis," David continued, "or data-driven decision making. It's only when you force your own *interpretation* onto those data points, that you're able to make sense of what you're looking at. Somebody at some point has to make some assumptions, and arrive at certain conclusions, based on those dots on the graph. You have to establish *causality*. Only then will the dots have meaning, and contribute to your understanding of what needs to be done.

"You have the facts in front of you in this case – the surveillance videos, the school's policies, your own eye-witness accounts. But those facts, alone, won't determine your course of action. You have to interpret the facts, fit them into your own paradigms, align them with your personal frames of reference, in order for them to have any meaning. And that interpretation, unavoidable, essential to your analysis, is the very thing that will drive your decision. Not the data itself."

Without looking up, her glasses perched on the end of her nose, Consuelo droned a monotone reply, her attitude snide and condescending.

"I'm sure we're all very interested to hear your theories on data-driven decision making, Mr. Mendoza. But in the interest of time, as my two colleagues here have already pointed out, I think we can forgo any further instruction along these lines. No matter how well intended."

David sat back in his chair and smiled. He'd made his point. No matter how much the assistant principal might wish to make it appear that her recommendations in this case, which no doubt were going to be highly condemnatory, would be entirely and impartially based on nothing other than empirical evidence and irrefutable analysis, in the end everyone knew that a large amount of subjectivity and personal bias would be impossible to avoid.

We three women sat in silence for a moment, trying to make up our minds as to what should be done. I turned and looked at the large portrait of Jesus on my wall. One of the benefits of running a charter school is the opportunity to bring my personal religious beliefs into the office, without fear of getting in trouble for it. Not everyone at EAST is a Christian or even a believer in God, which is completely fine with me. But my own choice is to proudly display, without apology or explanation, a beautiful painting of my Lord and Savior on my wall, for all to see. I want there to be no ambiguity whatsoever, as to where I stand.

I noticed that David, having caught the direction of my glance, was also looking at the framed artwork. For some reason, it made me glad.

"From where I sit," said Beth finally, "taking all of the circumstances into consideration, I have to say that at no time was anyone's safety in jeopardy, except in the sole case when Jake attempted to strike Mr. Mendoza in the face. And that act was precipitated by Mr. Mendoza's continuing to hold Jake in an obviously painful position, probably for more time than was warranted. I therefore conclude that Mr. Mendoza's actions were uncalled for and excessive, and that they should be subject both to censure and a penalty. That's my view, anyway."

"I completely agree with you," said Consuelo, still not looking at David.

I sighed. David didn't seem to be even slightly perturbed.

"Please understand," I said to him, "how reluctant I am to side with my colleagues on this. It pains me to the core. But we have policies to follow, and potential litigation to dodge."

He nodded. I turned to Beth.

"Please write up a formal warning, to be signed by each of us, based on the evidence brought to light in this meeting. Copy Bob on it. And have it on my desk before the end of the day."

Beth nodded. Everyone got up to leave.

"Wait a minute," I said. They turned to look at me. "Off the record, I want to state my true opinion. David, I'm so very glad you chose to join our staff. In the short time you've been here you've already made a world of difference. I want you to know how proud I am of you, for standing up to a bigot. Jake Powell will undergo a disciplinary meeting with us tomorrow, with his parents present as well. We'll see how that goes. And I'd like to add that I just hope that if I had been in the same situation, I'd have had the courage to stop that boy from removing the girl's hajib as well. One more thing. On a personal level, I completely disagree with the need to write you up at all. I think you did exactly the right thing."

David smiled.

"Thank you, Gloria," he said. "If I had it to do over again, I'm not sure I'd do anything differently."

Consuelo and Beth said nothing as they left my office. David turned to leave as well, and I grabbed him by the arm.

"You've not seen Consuelo's good side yet," I told him gently. "She truly is a wonderful person. She and I have known each other since childhood. We've always been best friends. She's a genuinely good person, David. One of the best I've ever met. I just wish the two of you had hit it off better."

He shrugged, shaking his head.

"I'm open to the possibility that she has some good in her," he said. "I just think our personalities are not compatible. Like water and oil. That's all."

Ellen poked her head in the doorway and said she needed to quickly discuss something related to an IEP for one of her kids. I saw her eyes light up and her cheeks blush when she realized David was in the room, and for a split second, I began to worry that I might end up with an inter-faculty romance to deal with. Never a good thing.

Then I saw the look of polite indifference, the utter lack of interest in David's eye, and I knew my concerns were unfounded. He nodded to her as she came in, and then he passed through the door, heading to the soggy parking lot for the first of his three days of suspension.

Ellen stepped inside, watching David as he walked away. I turned to open my mildew-speckled window blind, staring at the tiny raindrops as they dripped onto the street in front of the school, little pinpricks of agitation on the muddy surfaces of the puddles that were forming all around.

"Looks like it's shaping up to be another beautiful day," I said.

Ellen grinned.

"I know, right?" she said.

CHAPTER 19

DAVID

December 11.

Take heed to yourselves: If thy brother trespass against thee, rebuke him; and if he repent, forgive him.

Luke 17:3

I'M NOT sure whether last month's incident in the cafeteria hurt, or helped.

I couldn't care less about getting written up. I know they like me here, and my job's not in jeopardy. At all. I put my three days of suspension to good use, buying some nice house plants to help get me through the winter, spending some time in the library looking for good mysteries to read, reaching out to my son and daughter in Philadelphia. Good times.

Jake definitely behaves better in class, now. At least he doesn't keep making outbursts and disrupting everything. He sits there looking at me in silence, brooding, sometimes turning and whispering to Andrew, with a smirk on his face. He does well enough on the tests, and his writing's not horrible, so I've decided to let him glide through for now, without pushing him to participate in class discussions. He's still nursing his emotional wounds, and I recognize the need to allow him time to heal, without humiliating him in front of his peers.

The assistant principal apparently felt no hesitancy or qualms in her write-up of me. It was ten pages, more detailed than I would've believed, and highly critical of my actions in the lunchroom. I took it all in stride, though. I knew the school had no intention of actually disciplining me, let alone firing me, and this write-up was merely to make sure they'd covered their bases, in the off-chance of a lawsuit. Still, the words were biting, replete with venom and veiled insults. There was not a single positive thing said about me in the entire report.

After school today, in the pouring rain, I backed out of my parking spot quickly, in a hurry to be on my way. I turned too sharply, too soon, and my front bumper dented and scraped the passenger door of the silver Prius next to me.

After rolling my eyes and searching through my glovebox for a pen and a sticky pad, I dashed out a note with my name, phone number and an apology, saying I would take care of repairing the dented door myself. I didn't bother calling anyone to report the accident, since my insurance had lapsed. There'd be no point.

I was in a particularly sour mood when I drove home, after that.

CHAPTER 20

CONSUELO

December 19.

It was cold and rainy outside. Miserable.

I scanned a copy of the bill, from the body shop, and added it to a short mp4 snippet of a parking-lot surveillance video showing the moment David Mendoza's car swiped my own. I attached both of these to my email, together with instructions for him to pay me in full in the next three days, since I'd spent my entire Christmas budget, and more, on the repair.

I'd been planning on getting matching sets of parkas and boots for Alfredo and the kids, but unless Mr. Mendoza reimbursed me quickly, it wasn't going to happen. Somehow that creep had managed to ruin my family's Christmas, on top of everything else. Not to mention that I would've been able to finish my paperwork on curriculum redesign days earlier, if I'd not had to take my car into the shop.

It was the last day before Christmas break.

I spent an hour swimming laps, late in the afternoon. Then I headed upstairs to gather my curriculum redesign papers, which I'd left in Jennifer's room, after consulting with her and several other teachers in the English wing, on their class outlines for the upcoming semester. Thanks to Mr. Mendoza, I now had to work on the redesign at home, over the holiday, because I'd run out of time to finish it at school.

With my stack of papers and binders carefully balanced in both hands, I made my way to the elevator, barely poking a finger out from under the stack, trying to reach the down button, just as the door was closing. Someone else was in it already. I stuck my foot in the doorway, causing the elevator to reopen. I stepped inside.

CHAPTER 21

DAVID

December 19.

How long shall I take counsel in my soul, having sorrow in my heart daily? how long shall mine enemy be exalted over me?

Psalm 13:2

NOT ONLY DID she have the gall to stick me with a bill for $1,435 six days before Christmas; she included video footage of the incident, in her email. As if I might otherwise try to deny culpability and weasel my way out of it, the written confession in my little note notwithstanding. Talk about pouring salt into the wound.

Of all the cars I could've dented on that rainy day when I was leaving the parking lot, it had to be hers. Of course. Murphy's Law.

Where was I going to come up with that kind of money? School teachers aren't rich, needless to say. And her terms were that I pay it, in full, in the next three days. December 22. She gave me her email address and told me to PayPal her the amount. The gall.

I needed some time to breathe.

I'd been meaning to shop for new car insurance since moving to northern California, knowing the price would be different with my new zip code. In the process I'd received several quotes, but I'd unfortunately also allowed my previous insurance to lapse. So I had no coverage. Nothing to take care of the horrific damage I'd inflicted on Consuelo's innocent little car. The money was going to have to come out of my own pocket. And my bank account was mostly depleted, after the costs of moving up here a few months ago.

Not only that, Jake Powell hadn't spoken to me, not even once, since the incident in the cafeteria. At least he stayed far away from Fadila, now. As for her, she and her brother seemed happy enough, though neither of them ever spoke up in class much. But I was getting worried about Jake. We hadn't hit it off really well, but as long as he was a student of mine, I was concerned about his wellbeing and his development. Especially if his newly-forming bad attitude was due, even in part, to the things I'd said and done to him earlier.

After school was out for the day, I stuck around for a while, grading some papers, getting ready for January. It wasn't like I had someone waiting at home for me to hurry and get there, anyway. I would've been just as happy to take the papers with me to grade them over the holiday, but the email from the assistant principal had me on edge.

I'd been planning on buying a $39 lower-balcony ticket to go to a live performance of Handel's Messiah, to be presented by the Eureka Symphony and the Eureka Symphony Chorus, the following evening. But the prospect of coming up with $1,435 on short notice had made me stressed about the depletion of my bank account, so I decided to stick around and grade papers at the school, instead. Having such a large bill hanging over my head would've spoiled my ability to enjoy the concert and ruined it for me, anyway.

It was early evening when I turned off the lights and closed my classroom door, heading for the elevator. The building was already dark, and empty. I stepped inside, absently pushing the first-floor button, waiting for the door to close. Out of the corner of my eye I saw a foot stick in, blocking the door, pushing it open again.

Of all people, Consuelo herself stood there, a stack of papers and binders in her hands. Yay. Her glance was only brief, but there was enough time in it for her to give me the evil eye. Cold as ice.

Since she wasn't looking at me as she stepped inside, I took the opportunity to give her the once-over. Definitely frumpy. About my age. Wedding ring on her finger. Hair up in a bun. Short. Pudgy around the middle; saggy everywhere else. Ugly clothes. Big glasses, perched on her nose. Pathetic.

Impatient, I pushed the button to close the door, then turned to the side and waited, not looking in her direction.

Dead silence.

No "hello," or "how are you," or "got plans for the holidays?" No greeting whatsoever. No acknowledgement of my existence. No discussion of that egregious car repair bill of hers. Just the intense discomfort of being in such a confined space together, even if it was only to be for a few seconds.

The door finally closed. The elevator began to descend.

Halfway down, it jolted to an abrupt stop, and the lights flickered and went out. Pitch black. Total darkness. I heard a sharp intake of breath from Consuelo, but nothing more.

"What did you do?" she said, after a minute.

"What did *I* do?" I asked. "I didn't do anything."

She sighed loudly.

"Well?" she said. "Are you going to push the emergency button? Or do we just get to stand here for a while?"

"I don't know which button it is."

"Move out of the way," she said, and I could hear her putting down her stack of papers. I stepped back from the control panel and heard her pushing various buttons. Then it sounded like she was opening something.

"Strange," she said.

"What?"

She didn't answer. I heard more fiddling, and touching, and even a bit of pounding.

"Get out your cell phone," she said.

"It's in my car." I often left it there. It was sometimes too much of a distraction in class, when I was trying to teach.

"A lot of good it's going to do you, sitting out in your car."

"Why don't you get out yours?"

"Battery's dead," she said. "I already tried."

"A lot of good it'll do you, if you don't even bother to keep it charged."

"Smart guy."

"Isn't there supposed to be an emergency phone?"

"Already tried it. No dial tone."

"Maybe you did it wrong. Let me try."

"Be my guest."

I heard her stepping away from the panel, and I moved forward and tried every single button, pushing them multiple times. Nothing. One of the buttons was on a latch that popped open a small cabinet, though, beneath the panel. I reached inside and felt a telephone receiver. No dial tone. I tried several times to call. No use.

I stood on tiptoes and reached toward the ceiling panels, pushing upwards, trying to find a loose one. Consuelo's words put a stop to my efforts.

"No way to escape, from the top. It's sealed, for safety. People die when they try to get out of stuck elevators."

"Then I'll pry open the door."

"Won't work. That's how people get decapitated. We're between floors. Can't be opened."

She slipped off her shoes and, taking one of them into her hand, began to tap her heel against the elevator door, knocking, hoping someone would hear.

"I'm pretty sure we were the last ones in the building," I said.

"Right. So why don't you just stay there in your little corner and stop jabbering, and just do nothing, ok? I'll go ahead and work on getting us out of here."

If my face turned red, she didn't see it. I stepped toward the door and tried to wedge my fingers inside the gap, pulling for all I was worth. It didn't budge.

"Told you."

Feeling a bit panicked, I started to jump up and down, shouting for help.

"Don't do that. Not gonna help."

Being stuck in an elevator on the day before Christmas break was bad enough. Being locked in it with Consuelo was a thousand times worse. I could feel that I was sweating. Mild claustrophobia was setting in.

"Is anyone going to be in the building," I asked, "between now and the end of the holiday?"

"Abdullah might come in, to check on things. He's the head custodian."

"I know who he is."

"We can be quiet, and listen for him. But you're gonna have to stop jumping up and down like an idiot."

I stood there and thought about my own family situation. Would anyone know I was missing? My own two children, grown and married, were both living in the Philadelphia area. They'd probably call on Christmas day. But they'd have no idea I wasn't home, or why. They'd be too caught up in their own holiday activities, with their own kids. My grandchildren.

My own parents were dead. My older brother spoke to me no more frequently than once a year. And my new neighbors in Eureka hardly knew anything about me, or my habits. I realized with a sinking feeling that there wasn't a soul in the world who would know, or care, that I was locked up in this elevator with this crazy woman. I turned in her direction. She was still tapping on the door with her shoe.

"Do you have family?" I said. "Someone who'll notice you're missing?"

"Yeah."

She didn't elaborate, but I didn't need her to. I was relieved to know that I wouldn't be spending the entire holiday here, with her. Someone would no doubt come for us, but maybe not until the next day.

I sat down, unsure how I was going to pass the time without going insane. I heard Consuelo sitting down a minute later, across from me. I tried to make conversation.

"Are you cold?"

"Nope."

"I can't understand," I said, "why the emergency phone isn't working. Even with the power out, it should still be functional."

No response.

We sat there in silence. It was hard to tell how much time had passed; maybe twenty minutes. My stomach growled, loudly. In the confined space it sounded like a freight train.

"Sorry."

"We may be exposed," she said, "to biological functions substantially more conspicuous than that, before our time here is done."

I realized that my bladder was already feeling full, but said nothing about it. Another silent pause. Ten or fifteen minutes.

"It's almost like someone deliberately sabotaged it," I said, thinking out loud. "Like they not only shut off power to the elevator, but also disconnected the emergency button and the emergency phone. On purpose."

"Please don't talk to me. I'm trying to get some sleep."

That was that. So much for trying to engage in any sort of conversation. Might as well be talking to a stone wall.

I lay back, stretching myself along one side of the compartment, trying to get comfortable.

I tossed and turned for the better part of an hour. Sleep was simply not going to be part of the equation. Not that night.

After trying each side of my body multiple times, I gave up and lay flat on my back, staring up into the darkness, in the direction of the ceiling, breathing softly, not moving. My thoughts began to drift, for some inexplicable reason, to the time when I'd pretended to go hunting for a bear, outside the cabin in the forest, while my childish wife had been cooking stew inside. I reached deep into the back of my mind, trying to remember what it had been like. So many years had come and gone. The memories were still there, but deeply buried. It took all of the concentration I could muster to pull them out.

Truly the human brain is an amazing thing. A computer to surpass all computers. An endless repository of as much data as we choose to fill it with, never reaching the point of satiety. An athlete might push his or her body to the confines of its absolute physical boundaries, but the brain has no such limitations. No one's brain ever gets filled to capacity. When we think our brains can't contain any more information, it's always because we're physically exhausted, not mentally filled. There's always room for more. And, it would seem, everything we ever put in there remains locked away on some synaptic shelf, to be accessed at any future point in our lives, if and when the proper stimulus presents itself.

The matchless capacity of the human brain is, in itself, a powerful witness of the reality of a Divine Creator.

More than an hour passed. I shifted onto my side, completely uncomfortable on the hard floor. The reality of the hopelessness of our situation in that elevator was sinking in.

I heard Consuelo sigh, loudly, several times. Then everything was silent, for quite a while. Maybe another hour. It was impossible to tell; I had no watch.

I tried not to focus on my bladder.

Perhaps Consuelo thought I'd fallen asleep at that point, but I was actually wide awake, aware of the tiniest little noises. But the sound I heard, a few minutes later, took me by complete surprise.

She was crying. Very softly, trying not to make any noise, no doubt hoping I wasn't awake to hear it. Little sniffles, coupled with constricted breathing through a tight throat, and the telltale sounds of her own efforts to muffle her sobs and shudders.

I thought about saying something to her, but decided against it. What was there to say? I was sure that any pity from me would be the last thing on earth she'd want. Best just to let her think I was sleeping.

Sometime later, she brought her tears under control. After that, she turned to me and spoke, and I realized that she was aware that I'd been awake the entire time. That I knew she'd been crying.

"I wish you'd never come to this school."

Her voice was bitter. It was no secret that she detested me, but hearing her say it so directly was still unsettling.

"I wish you'd just stayed down there. In L.A., where you belong. You don't fit in, up here. It's not your place. From the day I met you, you've given me nothing but heartache and grief."

What did she want from me? An apology? Wasn't going to happen.

"The fact that I'm here in this elevator at all," she went on, "is entirely your fault. I was on track to finish my work, before the holiday, so I could spend Christmas with my family, without having to worry about unfinished business at the school. Thanks to you, I've now had to spend a significant amount of time in the body shop, overseeing the repair and repainting of my door. So I didn't have time to finish the project I was working on, after all. I had to go upstairs to pick it up, to take it home with me. That's the reason why I'm in this elevator, right now. I should be sitting down to dinner with Alfredo and the kids. Instead, I'm stuck in this awful place. With you."

"Did you call for prices," I said, "from all the different body shops in town? And then did you pick the most expensive one, just to spite me? Because $1,435 is way too much money for a bit of a bend and a scrape along your passenger door. I would've found a place to fix it for half that price."

"If you think, after the things you've done to me, that I'd actually entrust the repair of my vehicle to you, I obviously haven't made my thoughts on the subject clear enough. I seriously considered taking you to small claims court, to sue not only for the repair bill but also for the emotional damage you've inflicted. The dollar amount, as it is, is too small."

"Emotional damage? Seriously? You seem tougher than that."

"I am. That was why I didn't take you to court. But there ought to be a law against sheer *stupidity*. Because if there were, I think I could get enough money out of you to cover my whole retirement."

I had no desire to continue this pointless argument, but she went on anyway.

"Don't you dare try to worm your way out of paying that bill, either. You've already ruined my Christmas. The damage to my car was entirely caused by you. I don't suppose you're a responsible enough motorist to actually carry liability insurance, are you? No. Didn't think so. So you're gonna have to cough up the funds, from whatever source you can. I've given you three days, which I think is more than adequate. I'm determined to still do the last-minute Christmas shopping I'd hoped to get done a week earlier. I *need* the money."

I said nothing. After a few minutes, she continued.

"You seem like the kind of guy who has a red MAGA cap at home, sitting in a place of honor on a lofty shelf somewhere, waiting to be worn by you to some obnoxious sporting event. Am I right? I have no doubt in my mind *at all* that you voted for Trump. Tell me I'm wrong."

I didn't say anything for a long time, but finally I couldn't keep my silence.

"I voted third party. Libertarian."

"Hah!" she said, mocking me. "The marijuana guy, who had no idea there was even a place in the world called Aleppo. You voted for *that* guy, did you? Nice."

I didn't respond. I tried to put her out of my brain, to get some sleep. My bladder was full, my body was sore from trying to rest on the hard floor, and my companion for the next untold hours seemed determined to deride me. It was going to be a long night.

CHAPTER 22

CONSUELO

December 19.

I was bored out of my mind.

What had I done, to deserve the infernal torment I was undergoing in that pernicious little metal prison? Sleep was not a possibility. I got up and did some pushups, then several sets of sit-ups, longing for the cleansing that can only come from a nighttime swim in an empty pool. My feet kept coming up during the sit-ups, but I wasn't about to ask the loser next to me to come over and hold them down for me. As if.

But I *had* to have something to do. The monotony was driving me bonkers. I wanted to belittle my fellow inmate, berate him, mock him, make him feel ridiculous. Without giving it a lot of thought, I resorted to an old standby of mine: trivia.

"Who wrote *The Screwtape Letters?*" I said, completely out of the blue. There was a momentary silence.

"Huh?"

"*The Screwtape Letters.* Or don't you know?"

"Lewis."

Too easy. I'd forgotten that he was an English teacher.

"Ok," I said, "um . . . what's the biggest dam on the Nile?"

"Aswan."

"Uh-huh. All right, what's the name of the most radioactive isotope on earth?"

"Polonium 210."

I was floored. Maybe this guy wasn't so airheaded, after all. Even if he did vote for Gary Johnson.

I decided I was going to stump him. Not with some obscure question no one could possibly know the answer to, but with something that would make him feel ashamed, for not knowing the correct answer, and for realizing that he should. Before I could ask him another question, though, he tossed one out at me. Completely unexpected.

"What's the only bird known to sometimes fly backwards?"

Easy one.

"Hummingbird."

"Who was the first Tudor monarch of England?"

"Let's see . . . Henry the . . . Seventh."

"Correct. What's the national sport of Japan?"

"Sumo."

My years of watching *Jeopardy* were paying off, so far. But David was keeping up with me. I upped the ante, trying to think of harder questions, lobbing them at him in rapid succession, one after another.

"What's the so-called 'dead man's hand?' In poker?"

"Um . . . two aces and two eights."

He did well, much better than I would've thought he'd have done. And for every question he answered, he sent one right back at me.

It passed the time; what can I say? It was actually fun. For both of us, I think. Something we had in common, after all. Who would've thought?

We went on that way for what must've been an hour, at least. Maybe two. We covered dozens of topics. I discovered at some point that both of us seemed to avoid all sports-related questions. We also steered clear of topics involving alcoholic drinks. Funny.

"Where'd you go to school?" I asked him without thinking, surprising myself as much as I must've surprised him. He hesitated for a moment.

"Is that a trivia question?"

"No. You . . . don't have to answer, if you don't want to."

"UCLA. Bachelor's in English Language Arts. You?"

"Berkeley. Master's in chemistry. USC before that."

"I see," he said. "So that's the reason for all the chemistry questions, then."

"Hey, I gave you lots of other topics, too."

"True enough. And I suppose I threw a fair number of literature ones, at you."

"Any kids living at home?"

"No. I raised two children. A daughter and a son. Both are grown, and gone now. Married, with children of their own. They live in Pennsylvania."

"Together?"

"No. Opposite sides of Philadelphia. About an hour apart."

"Oh," I said. "I have two kids at home. Jackie, who's nine, and Tanner, who'll be seven in January."

"Nice. I'll bet they're excited for Christmas. Any pets?"

"Brutus. Golden retriever. Nicest dog in the world. Does your wife work?"

"My wife left me, for a guy on a motorcycle. It's been a number of years now."

I didn't know what to say to that: I'm sorry? Too bad? Tough break? I chose not to say anything.

Then he spoke again. Changed the subject. Totally random.

"Knock-knock!"

He said it suddenly, as if to test me. To gauge whether he'd really begun to win me over as a friend, I supposed. I took the bait.

"Who's there?"

"Olive Tupe."

"Olive Tupe who?"

"You do? No kidding. Why, *ah* love to poo, too!"

He snickered, then was quiet.

I sat there, stunned by the imbecile quality of his inane little joke.

Then, all at once, for reasons completely unknown to me even now, as I write these words, the thing struck me as absurdly funny. I covered my mouth with my hand, trying not to let myself do anything embarrassing.

He let out another little snicker, and that was all it took. The floodgates burst. I exploded into raucous, uncontrolled laughter. I couldn't stop.

He was laughing along with me, and after a minute I could feel the tears, trickling out of the corners of my eyes. The harder I tried to recover my composure, the sillier my mirth became. It was the deepest, most powerful succession of belly-laughs I'd experienced since I'd been a kid.

"Knock-knock!" I spouted gleefully, fighting to regain enough control simply to get the words out.

"Who's there?"

"Interrupting cow."

"Interrupting . . ."

Before he could say the words, "cow who," I shouted, "*Moo!*"

He snorted and continued to laugh, even louder than before. So did I.

I tried to recall all the jokes Jackie had brought home from school and shared with me over the past year. They'd never been really funny to me, before. Now, each one seemed to be the most hilarious bit of comedy I'd ever encountered.

"Knock-knock."

"Who's there?"

"Cash."

"Cash who?"

"No, thank you. But have you got a peanut?"

Boisterous laughter from both David and me.

"Knock-knock."

"Who's there?"

"Europe."

"Europe who?"

"No, I'm not! *You're* a poo."

We kept it up, laughing like crazy fools, and for the next fifteen minutes each of us was racking our brains to remember every joke we'd ever been told, no matter how silly or whimsical. They were ludicrous, puerile, juvenile. And each one made us laugh harder than the one before.

"You're killing me," I said. "I *really* need to go to the bathroom."

"So do I," he said. "You keep making me laugh. Not sure how much longer I can hold it."

"If you lose control of your bladder," I said, "I'm not going to hold it against you, considering the circumstances. But stay on your side of the elevator. Please."

"Fair enough," he said. "We'll see how long I can hold out. Ok. Say these words three times in a row, as fast as you can: *one smart feller, he felt smart; two smart fellers, they both felt smart.*"

A tongue twister. Fine. I gave it a shot.

"One smart feller," I began.

"Faster!" David said.

I sped up.

"One smart feller, he felt smart. Two smart fellers, they both smelt . . . they both smelt . . ."

I couldn't go any further. I thought I was going to burst. What on earth did I find so uproariously funny about such silly bathroom humor? But I couldn't stop laughing. And if I'm going to be completely honest here, it felt good. Really good.

After that it was easier for us to talk. The ice between us – and heaven knows there had been a lot of it – was finally broken.

We discussed the students in his different classes, and other kids in the school. We talked about life in Eureka – what to do, where to eat, what things to see, where to shop.

Over time, the conversation grew more personal – how we viewed things, what we hoped to get out of life, what really mattered to us. We went on talking, into what must have been the wee hours of the morning.

I realized, at one point, that being locked up in that tiny space with David Mendoza didn't end up being the tragedy that I'd dreaded. Quite the opposite. It occurred to me that I was having a great time. I no longer even felt such a need for sleep. We talked and laughed and shared things, as though we'd been the best of friends. It was wonderful. So much better than the way everything had been between us, before. Amazing, the difference a few hours can make.

I didn't want to bring up any issues from our past. Nothing that might jeopardize this new-found friendship. But I couldn't continue to ignore the little voice inside of me which kept prompting me to say something.

"I just want you to know," I said quietly, after a brief pause in our conversation, "that I very much appreciate the way you handled it, when Jake Powell was trying to take off Fadila's hijab. I'm so glad you stopped him."

He sounded surprised.

"Really? I wouldn't have known that, based on that meeting in Gloria's office last month. And your write-up."

"I know. I'm sorry. I . . . got the wrong impression, I think. When I met you. By the way - it looked like karate, when you twisted Jake's arm the way you did. I suppose you're a practitioner of some sort of martial art?"

"There's no doubt that I misjudged you, too," he said. "And yes, I've been doing taekwondo for years. Oh, and also, for the record, I absolutely do plan to pay you the $1,435. As soon as we get out of here. I'll Paypal it to you."

"About that," I said, feeling a bit nervous. "Full disclosure – it was my cousin that did the repair. He actually *owns* the body shop. He was gonna charge me $300. I told him to mark it way up. To do extra work on the door, to make everything absolutely perfect. Like new. I made a point of paying him the full $1,435, so that you'd have to reimburse that same amount to me. But he would've been totally happy to do it for $300."

"You're kidding," David said. "I can't believe you did that."

"Sorry." I suddenly felt so ashamed. "The truth is, I didn't even care about the damage to the dumb door. I'm not finicky, that way. No big deal, really. I just saw it as a way of . . . it was, like, an opportunity to take a swipe at you, if you know what I mean. I'm truly sorry."

It was quiet for a bit. I didn't dare say anything else about it.

"So . . . is it going to be $300, or $1,435?" he asked.

"I'm going to talk to my cousin. He'll keep $300 out of what I gave him, and he'll give the rest back. And my penance for doing the evil deed of telling him to mark it up in the first place, will be to eat the $300 cost myself. So don't worry about it. I'll take care of it. Sorry I tried to take advantage of you like that. But this one's gonna be on me. No charge."

"No," he said, "I caused the damage. I'll be responsible to pay for the repair. But if your cousin will take $300, then that's how much I'll give you. Much better than $1,435. Which means I'll actually have a bit of money left in my account after all. For last-minute shopping. And I was worried about going to *The Messiah* tomorrow night. Now I'll know I can afford the cost of a ticket."

"Are you talking about the Eureka Symphony?" I said. "I've already got tickets, for me and my family. We go every year. It's outstanding."

"You like Baroque composers?"

"Anyone with enough genius to write *Surely he hath borne our griefs*, *Water Music*, and *Sarabande*, is ok in my book."

"Agreed," he said. "Maybe I'll see you guys there, then. Where will you be sitting?"

"Lower balcony."

"You think there are any seats left?"

"Maybe. But *The Messiah* is always hugely popular."

He didn't say anything, so I spoke again, fascinated by how our conversation in the darkness of the elevator had become so casual and intimate.

"You'll just be going by yourself, then?" I asked. "Alone?" I tried to sound casual.

"It's not like there's anyone in the area who knows me," he said, and I realized how lonely it must've been for him to be living all by himself. To not have any real friends.

"Maybe we'll bump into each other at the concert," I said. "What are your plans for Christmas?"

"What do you mean?"

"Are you going anywhere? Going to be with anyone?"

"No."

"Do you even have a Christmas tree?"

"It's been years since I've put one up. Not much point in it, living on my own and all. Holidays aren't really geared for single people, you know."

I sensed that he could tell I was thinking about what he'd said. He kept quiet. Finally I spoke up.

"That's not right," I said, not sure where I was going with the comment. "No one should have to spend Christmas day alone."

On a whim, I went on, before I'd had too much time to think about what I was saying.

"Tell you what. At my house, the kids and I are going to wake up early – way too early, in my opinion – and they'll be done with opening their presents by ten o'clock, if not before. We're going to have an early Christmas dinner. Maybe two in the afternoon, or something. Why don't you come over then? Have dinner with us. It'll be fun."

I tried not to sound too eager, but I was prepared to insist that he say yes, if he should waver. What else was he gonna be doing on Christmas, anyway? I realized that I was actually looking forward to having him there, with us. I thought the kids would appreciate his personality, and I envisioned him eating my food and passing the time with my family. It put a smile on my face.

There was a lull in the conversation. Obviously he was mulling over his answer to my invitation. Should I say something else? Encourage him in some other way? I really wanted him to come. Finally he spoke up.

"Consuelo," he said, and I liked the way it sounded when he pronounced my name, "a day ago, before all this 'excitement' in the elevator, if anyone had proposed that I spend my Christmas afternoon in *your* home, of all places, I would've laughed off the suggestion as completely insane. But I've come to realize, in these past hours, that my initial impression of you was wrong. You're much more of a kindred spirit than I would've thought. It was probably the trivia questions that did it. So yes, I'd be honored to spend Christmas afternoon with you and your family. And thanks for being thoughtful enough to invite me."

In the darkness, he couldn't see the smile on my face. Nor was he aware of the flush of warmth that was spreading through my body.

What on earth had I been thinking, inviting *David Mendoza* to my house for Christmas dinner? Had I completely lost my mind? But what was done, was done. No turning back.

What was I going to cook? I hoped he liked Mexican food. That was pretty much the only thing I ever made. And what was I going to wear? Would the kids like him? And for that matter, what was Alfredo going to think about all of this?

I'd been assuming that David's views on fundamental things, like the birth of Jesus Christ, were similar to those of my own family. What if I'd been wrong? What if he was a non-believer? Did it matter?

Because Christmas, for me, wasn't just about Santa and candy canes and stockings. For my family, there'd always been a deeper, more spiritual element to the holiday. What if David didn't share that view? Was this going to end up being horribly awkward?

Just when my doubts and second thoughts were at a peak, he blindsided me with another question, the way he'd already done more than once, completely out of the blue.

"What church do you go to?"

I opened my mouth to answer, but at that very moment the lights in the elevator flickered and turned back on. There was a shudder, and I could feel that we were moving down, to the first floor. The door slowly began to open.

We were free.

CHAPTER 23

DAVID

December 20.

And the fruit of righteousness is sown in peace of them that make peace.

James 3:18

WE BLINKED, in the brightness of the light. It was daytime outside. Probably morning. We'd spent the whole night, then. And the building still seemed to be empty.

Consuelo was pushing her hair up, tucking a couple of loose strands behind her ears, trying not to look unkempt. As if that mattered to me. I glanced over at her and smiled, and I saw that although my initial visual assessment had been accurate, there was also something I'd missed, before. Her clothes were indeed dowdy and baggy, and she was short and plump, though with all her layers it was hard to tell where the clothing ended and her body began. Her glasses were thick, connected to a chain which she wore like an ugly necklace. Her wedding ring looked particularly tawdry, almost like it was made out of plastic. But something about her face was nice. Her eyes were warm, sincere. Genuine.

She flashed a shy smile at me, and I smiled back. I liked her. It was such a compelling transformation. As though my worst enemy were about to become one of my best friends. An early Christmas present for me.

I helped her gather up her papers and binders in spite of the urgent pain from my swollen bladder, and we heard footsteps coming from down the hallway. Abdullah approached us, a look of concern on his face, his eyes shifting between the elevator and the two of us.

"How long . . ?" he said, pointing.

"Since last night," I said.

He was frowning, shaking his head.

"Very strange," he said with his thick accent. "I think, last night someone come into thee elevator closet. Into thee control room, you know?"

"Yes," said Consuelo.

"I think . . . I think he disconnect thee elevator telephone line, yes? And he disconnect power to thee elevator. I do not know who would do this thing?"

"You're right," Consuelo agreed. "It is strange. I'll examine the video footage and see who it was. Anyway, thanks for turning the power back on and letting us out, Abdullah."

He nodded and went off down the hallway. I looked at Consuelo.

"Who else, besides him, has access to the elevator control room?" I asked.

"No one, as far as I know. Probably Gloria, and Beth. No one else, I would think. There's a passcode. You have to enter it, on a lock on the door."

"What about the other janitors? Would they know the code?"

"Possibly."

"Any chance that Abdullah himself would've caused the outage? Is it possible that he's maybe trying to make it look like someone else did it?"

"We'll know after I look at the surveillance video," she said.

I nodded.

She seemed so much more businesslike, now that we were in the daylight again, back in our former roles. We headed down the hallway together, in the direction of the faculty parking lot, both of us walking gingerly, desperately needing to stop along the way to make frantic use of the restrooms.

When I emerged minutes later, much relieved, she was standing there in the hall, waiting for me.

"Pretty quick," I said.

"I've had years of practice," she said with a smile. She looked *so* much better when she smiled, I decided.

She turned and headed off toward the parking lot. I went with her, beginning to wonder whether her Christmas invitation to me had been a fluke, something she now regretted. Maybe she hadn't really meant it. Perhaps the time we'd spent together in the darkness had held more meaning for me than it had for her, after all.

"I want to thank you for making my time in that jail cell bearable," she said, interrupting my thoughts as she walked alongside me. "I think

I'm only going to be taking the stairs from now on. No more elevators. For the rest of my life."

"Was it as bad as all that?" I asked, smiling at her. She turned and looked at me, unable to keep a straight face.

"Worse," she said. "At least, at first. But after a while I began to see that things were going to turn out all right, after all."

She beamed at me after that, a full-on, tooth-flashing grin, and I was floored by how pretty her smile was. How had I missed that before?

"Oh," she said as I opened the door and we stepped outside, "by the way. Be careful to watch where you're going, when you back up. You may not have known about it, but this parking lot happens to be notorious for accidents. Fender benders, scraped doors. You know what I mean. Lots of inattentive drivers around here, I guess. Some of them are *very* inattentive."

There was a twinkle in her eye. I rolled my eyes and nodded.

"See you on the twenty-fifth," she said, heading across the empty lot toward her Prius. "Two o'clock. I'll text you my address."

My heart skipped a beat. She'd meant it, then. And she didn't seem to have any regrets.

All the way home, even though I was dying for want of a shower and a bite to eat, I couldn't wipe the silly grin off my face.

CHAPTER 24

CONSUELO

December 25.

It was a nice Christmas morning, though the kids seem to be growing a bit more spoiled with each passing year. The whole tradition of ripping open a big pile of presents seems to have evolved into a self-indulgent orgy of materialism and entitlement. It's all about me, me, me.

But Alfredo was in a good mood anyway, which made me happy. He's been down for so much of this past year. I'm glad he seems to be finally coming around.

The kids were understandably freaked out last week, when I'd been stuck in the elevator and hadn't come home until the following morning. They were frantic. Alfredo had called the police, along with all of our relatives, in a desperate search. It's nice to be loved. There were hugs and tears when I got home, and everyone insisted that I tell them what it was like to be stuck in a dark metal box all night.

My favorite part of the holiday, I think, was the night before Christmas, when we sat together and read through the second chapter of the gospel of St. Luke, in the New Testament. Some of the most beautiful, evocative prose ever written. I thought, sitting there with Alfredo and the kids, that I should've invited David to be with us on Christmas Eve as well, but then I thought better of it. Might be a bit too weird.

But I have to admit that my mind kept wandering to him, during the week leading up to Christmas day. I'd looked all around at the concert, but I hadn't caught sight of him. Had he stayed home, after all? Maybe. But if he *had* been at the concert, had he tried to see if I was there, the way I'd been looking around the room for him?

I had to smile to myself when I realized, in the kitchen on Christmas afternoon as I was hurrying to add a few finishing touches to the large dinner I'd made, how disappointed I'd been not to have seen him. What was it about the man that was making me let down my guard so much? How was it that he'd managed to counteract my willful misanthropy? No matter. It was about time someone had knocked me off that particular high horse, anyway. Now I found myself almost giddy to welcome him into my home. I was genuinely hoping he would like my cooking. And that he had a taste for Mexican food. Given his last name, I was fairly confident he did.

My mind wandered again to the elevator incident. The video footage had given no indication of anyone entering the building, other than Abdullah. No record of who it might've been who shut off the power and disconnected the emergency phone.

Ours is an elevator that provides access to the back parking lot. There are three options – second floor, first floor, and ground, which opens to an outside, basement-level area for loading freight. The elevator's secure from the outside; you can't open it without a key. But from the inside, simply pushing the "G" button would take you to the ground floor, where the door would open and you could exit the building. Why that would matter to anyone, though, wasn't clear to me.

I'd met with Sally Ringerton, a police detective, the day before Christmas eve, apologizing profusely for intruding on her time during the holiday season. She told me not to worry, saying she was on the clock either way, and that she'd rather have spent her time doing something constructive.

We examined the surveillance recordings in my office, and she paused and restarted them at various points, drawing my attention to some evidence I'd missed, which suggested that someone had carefully edited one of them, splicing together two segments with a thirty-minute time-counter gap in between.

"I'm not going to lie," she said to me, concerned. "If this is what I think it is, someone's up to no good here. Someone who's devious enough to steal, and then make a copy, of your master key. Someone who knows how to access your surveillance video files, and edit them to hide his or her identity. Do you have any idea who might've done this? Any reason why someone might want to access, and alter, this stuff?"

I gave her the names of the people who had master keys. She wasn't overly concerned about Beth or Gloria, but she spent some time focusing on Abdullah, wanting to know his personality, his background, his tendencies. When I mentioned how he'd spit on Jake Powell that day in the cafeteria, her suspicions grew.

"I really don't think he would do something like this," I said. "He seemed as surprised to find us locked in that elevator as we were."

"He might've killed the power and disconnected the phone without realizing anyone was still in the building," she said.

"Yeah, but why would he want to do that?"

"To test it. To see if anyone would notice, or come in and try to fix it. The holiday break would be the perfect time to do that."

"You're saying maybe he wanted to know if he could use that knowledge on some future date? Like for an act of terrorism or something?"

"These are scary times," she said, leaning back in her chair. "I'm not accusing him of anything. But when it comes to school safety, nothing's off the table. Everyone's a suspect. Even you."

I'd nodded my understanding, still inwardly doubting that Abdullah could possibly have been the person who'd deliberately shut off power to the elevator.

These thoughts were swirling in my head when there was a knock at the front door. My heart fluttered in spite of myself, and I wiped my hands on my apron and let David in. He was smiling, nicely dressed, and every bit a gentleman.

He was very complimentary of my cooking: holiday tamales, *chiles rellenos*, slices of *carne asada*, Mexican rice, and homemade refried beans, with fresh salsa and steaming corn tortillas and pickled jalapenos on the side. Maybe he was only being polite; I don't know. But everything tasted good to me, and I think he genuinely liked it.

Alfredo and the kids inhaled every morsel I'd put on their plates, apparently without even stopping to taste it, but not before drowning it all under gallons of Habanera sauce, stuffing endless tortillas into their mouths as though they'd been forced to survive without food for a month. I was slightly embarrassed for them, but David took it all in stride, not seeming to mind in the least. Alfredo and the kids took to him almost at once, as I knew they would. Thankfully, none of the awkwardness I'd worried about ever materialized.

After eating, we retired to the living room. Alfredo soon excused himself to go take a nap somewhere, and Jackie and Tanner went off to play with their new toys, leaving me and David alone, to pick up where we'd left off, six days earlier. After a long chat we were interrupted by Jackie, who wanted to sing some Christmas carols with us. We sat around the piano and I played while we sang together. The time seemed to pass too quickly. David had a nice voice. After that I went into the kitchen and made some Abuelita's hot chocolate with cinnamon, which we sat and sipped together while we watched the rain drizzling outside.

Tanner came in and begged for a mug of his own, which I gave him. He slurped it noisily, with a spoon, after which he demanded that the four of us play Telestrations together. David was a bit sheepish about the prospect, worried that Alfredo might be hurt if we left him out.

"Do you think he might want to play it with us?" David asked.

"Nah," said Tanner. "Daddy's asleep. His naps go on for hours."

"It's true," I said. "He won't mind at all if we go ahead without him."

The game was a hoot. Jackie and Tanner saw to that, their silly drawings making the interpretation more than half the battle. We laughed and laughed, and then the kids went away and David and I talked some more.

Alfredo finally came out of hibernation, proposing to me that we eat some leftovers for supper together. It was getting dark outside, with no indication that the rain was ever going to let up, and I agreed that we should eat again.

The meal was quiet, with just the three of us. The kids weren't hungry at all. When we were done, David said he should go, and thanked me and Alfredo profusely for letting him spend his Christmas with our family.

I walked him to the door, and he suddenly seemed bumbling and uncomfortable in the extreme, not allowing himself to even look into my eyes. I wondered what I'd said or done to make him feel so uneasy. Must've been lingering pain from the horrible way I'd treated him previously, I decided.

I thanked him again for coming and told him to have a good night, as he stepped out into the rain.

CHAPTER 25

DAVID

December 25.

Judge not according to the appearance, but judge righteous judgment.

John 7:24

YOU'D THINK, after having been married twice, that I'd have, by now, a fairly solid grasp of the psychological makeup of women, and of their effect on me. Wrong.

Driving home, after spending all afternoon and evening at Consuelo's house, I didn't mind the rain, or the darkness, at all. I felt a warmth all over. I was beaming, happier than I'd felt since I didn't know when. I'd had a much, much better time with Consuelo's family than I'd thought I was going to.

She lived fifteen minutes north of town, in Arcata, close to Humboldt State. Her kids were as cute as could be, and seeing her in her own element, I was amazed to note how very different her persona was, compared with the front she put on in her job. At home, she let her hair down. Her clothes were different – a loose pair of sweats, an oversized sweatshirt. She was relaxed, smiling, witty. I couldn't believe the difference.

And as much as I'd love to say that her husband was a total jerk, or an idiot, he actually seemed to be a genuinely nice guy. A bit stiff and somber, perhaps, but he obviously doted on the children and was friendly and welcoming to me. I liked him. I wished I didn't, but I couldn't help it. I wasn't entirely sure what Consuelo had seen in him, but I had to agree that, all things considered, she'd chosen well.

CHAPTER 26

ELLEN

December 26.

Depressing. An entire year ahead of me, before Christmas rolls around again. What can I look forward to now? Summer break? Six months away. Yippee.

The kids seem to be going through a sugar let-down, today. Fine with me. I got my fill of them, yesterday. Let 'em sleep. Not that I don't love them, but sometimes, with them, a little bit goes a long way, if you know what I mean.

I'm really not one for excessive sentimentality. I'd take down the tree today, if I had the energy. Maybe tomorrow. But the holiday was good, because it was a disruption in the routine. A distraction from my otherwise mundane, extremely boring life.

Gloria called me today. Told me Consuelo was stuck with David Mendoza in the elevator, last week. *Overnight.* Scandalous.

I wish it had been me, instead of her. Talk about missed opportunities. To be confined to a dark elevator with that guy, for a whole night? I'm pretty sure I could've found a way to pass the time. Haha.

LOL.

CHAPTER 27

DAVID

January 6.

And he shall spread forth his hands in the midst of them, as he that swimmeth spreadeth forth his hands to swim:

Isaiah 25:11

I HAVE ONLY one New Year's resolution to make this year – to get my mind off of a particular co-worker, who happens to be married. Consuelo's already taken; I need to get my brain back, to focus on what I'm doing. Eliminate distractions.

Jennifer, my mentor, gave me some back-to-school pointers on how to handle discipline issues in my classes. I think she did it more out of duty than perceived need. She's younger than me, and less experienced, but she does her best, and she takes this mentorship seriously. More power to her.

Before she left, she invited me to go to the swimming pool with her tomorrow at 6 p.m., after the swim team's done with their practice. She said Eureka makes people get cabin fever in the extreme, with all the cold, rainy winter. The school's pool is brightly lit, and the walls, painted in warm orange and yellow tones, can have something of a therapeutic effect on people, she said. She confided that she suffers from SAD (seasonal affective disorder), and that swimming a few laps has never failed to brighten her spirits and recharge her batteries.

I accepted the invitation. Why not?

But when I turned to go, I saw that Ellen, the geography teacher, was just down the hall and had likely overheard our entire conversation. Is she going to show up at the pool, too? Her clumsy flirtation has become increasingly annoying to me, and obvious to everyone else. I don't know how to let her down gently without hurting her feelings.

Andrew came walking down the hall with Jake Powell, laughing over some shared joke until they saw me standing there. Instantly the levity stopped, and they walked past me, glaring, frowning, saying nothing.

At least Jake no longer torments Fadila. But it's unlikely that he'll ever be friendly to me again. I find myself strangely regretting the loss.

CHAPTER 28

JENNIFER

January 6.

I freely admit that an ulterior motive in my inviting David Mendoza to come swimming today was a desire to see the man in a bathing suit. As far as that goes, I'll only say that he didn't disappoint. For a middle-aged schoolteacher past his prime, he looked more like a fashion model than a high school instructor.

And he's always so nice, so accommodating. I'll be the first one to say that I'm super awkward as his mentor, advising him on things when he should be the one advising me. But he takes it all in stride, with humility and appreciation. Which makes him all the more endearing.

I felt a bit embarrassed in my own swimsuit, but he hardly seemed to notice me, after all. Nor did he pay any particular attention to Ellen, who's much cuter, and younger, than I am. She was already there when we arrived, giggling, chomping on a stick of gum, flirting and splashing around.

I started out by swimming a few laps with David, dove off the board a few times, and did some playful stunts – walking on my hands, swimming underwater, retrieving a pen from the bottom of the deep end – things like that. Then Consuelo came in.

CHAPTER 29

DAVID

January 6.

Lust not after her beauty in thine heart; neither let her take thee with her eyelids.

Proverbs 6:25

I TRIED NOT to be rude to Jennifer. She was the one who'd invited me, after all. I kept reminding myself to look over at her, notice what she was doing, smile at her. Not that this was a date, really. But still. I was supposed to be here *with her*.

But I couldn't take my eyes off Consuelo. No glasses; no hair bun; no frumpy, layered clothing. She wasn't a bit overweight. Not a bit. It had been all the clothes. Not that she had the body of a teenager. She was probably fifty, at least. But she definitely kept herself fit, no doubt from all the swimming. A fact which she chose to keep completely concealed from the rest of the world, apparently.

Her face, though, without the glasses, was the real thing that caught my eye. So warm. So beautiful. I had no idea. Why did she hide herself all day? What reason did she have for not letting everyone see what she had to offer? She was so much more beautiful, inside and out, than she allowed herself to be.

She waved at me briefly, then dove in and started doing her laps. Jennifer and I had been using the diving board. I switched to laps, in the lane next to Consuelo, and fell in behind her. Ever the competitive one, she saw what I was doing and picked up her pace a little. I started to go faster, too. Soon it was an all-out race, and when each of us reached the end of the pool, we turned and headed for the other side, locked neck-in-neck. Halfway across she started to gain a little, and by the time we reached the side, she was a full body-length ahead of me. Her head popped up out of the water, dripping, exultant, grinning from ear to ear. I'd never seen her smile so brightly.

In that moment, my heart melted.

I knew she was married. I knew my own self, my ethics, my personal moral code, my conscience. All of these things had been reinforced by my return to the religion of my youth, some years earlier, and my renewal of the commitments I'd made in my early years. I'd known in my heart that what I was doing was right, at the time. Making commitments that would last a lifetime, and beyond.

And even now, as I stood there in the water, looking at the woman who'd stolen my heart without so much as a single word, I was equally certain that I'd never do anything to betray the trust of her good husband or otherwise allow myself to grow emotionally or romantically attached to her. The invisible boundary between us could not have been more clearly marked. And I knew I would never cross it.

Nevertheless, my New Year's resolution to put her out of my mind flew out the window, at that moment. It would be impossible, moving forward, to deny the stirrings I felt within myself. It would be dishonest to try to persuade myself that I felt nothing for her. So I resolved to change my resolution. Rather than trying to force myself to forget her, I'd simply have to commit to only thinking of her in my most private, innermost thoughts. And to never, ever act on those thoughts, no matter what happened.

CHAPTER 30

FADILA

January 18.

Martin Luther King's birthday. He seems to have been a good guy, the Reverend Mr. King. A man who wasn't afraid to stand up for the oppressed, the disenfranchised, the marginalized. Like me.

I'm glad to be able to stay home from school today. Dad's home, too.

I worry about him, sometimes. He can be so loyal, so single-minded in his dedication to a cause. I worry that sometimes he's willing to throw reason, and caution, out the window. So I try to engage him in activities that will calm his mind, bring him back down to earth.

He likes being a janitor. It gives him the opportunity to undergo hours of nothing but monotonous physical activity, which drains his anxiety and helps him forget the troubles of his awful past.

In 2012, Hasan and I were just young kids living in Raqqa when our mother was forcibly taken away from us. We never learned who did it, or why. She simply wasn't there one night, when it was time for dinner. No one had seen her. We knew she hadn't gone off on her own; someone had kidnapped her. We never learned the reason. We never saw her again.

About a year after that, Dad was forced one sunny morning onto the top of a four-story building by a group of ISIL soldiers with machine guns. They made him stand in the back of a line up there on the roof, with about fifty other men - friends and neighbors, mostly. One by one, the captives were forced to the edge of the rooftop, where they were compelled to renounce their Christianity. Anyone who refused was thrown off.

By the time it was Dad's turn, there were already more than a dozen bodies on the unpaved street below him. Some were men he'd known. The dirt in the street was turning to mud, from their blood. The fact that my family happened to be muslim didn't make it any easier for him, even if there wasn't any reason to renounce a religion he didn't belong to. The emotional trauma from standing on the edge of that roof, looking down at the bodies of those who'd been unwilling to deny their God, was no less damaging. In some ways it would've been easier just to have been pushed off, with the rest of them.

We left Syria after that. Migrated to America, as political refugees.

I've often wondered what Martin Luther King would've said, if he'd been one of the ones on the rooftop that morning. He'd been a Christian minister, right? A reverend? Was it possible that he would've perhaps quietly renounced Jesus and praised Allah, to save his own skin? Something inside me wants to think that he wouldn't. After all, he ended up giving his life for a good cause, at least in a way. Didn't he?

I have to wonder what a kid like Jake Powell thinks about someone like Martin Luther King. Lately he's been pretending that he cares about me. Treating me civilly. Nicely. But it's all an act, I know. All for show. He's setting me up, trying to make me vulnerable. So he can pounce on me one of these days, in front of his friends. Ridicule me in some obscene, spectacular way. To save face, I suppose.

Only it's not going to happen. I'm onto him. The guy's obviously still nursing his wounds – his psychological scars – from the humiliation he got from Mendoza, months ago. He shouldn't have tried to take off my hijab. He'd gotten what was coming to him.

Even as I struggle to help my dad keep his emotions in check, Hasan seems to copycat him in everything he does, always taking his side. I think that maybe I worry about my brother, perhaps, even more than my dad. He's so serious, all the time. I love him and am grateful that he wants to protect me, but it's all I can do to keep him from taking things to the extreme. The day he heard about my encounter with Jake, he was ready to go kill him. Literally. Just like that. It was no easy task to talk him out of it.

I'm still secretly in love with Mendoza, btw. Probably now more than ever.

He'll never know. No one will ever know, except for whoever reads this.

But I find myself daydreaming, all the time, of a world with no one living in it but me and him. He takes care of me in that empty place, and loves me, and is respectful of my wishes and beliefs and traditions. And I know that if such a place actually existed and he and I were indeed its sole occupants, that's exactly how he would be.

It's just a foolish girl's fantasy. But I can dream, can't I? It's a free country, after all.

CHAPTER 31

CONSUELO

January 31.

I made David a cupcake for his birthday. Brought it in and gave it to him, between classes.

It was just a small gesture, but he seemed more affected, and grateful, than I would've imagined. I wondered whether there was anyone who'd recognize that it was his special day. Anyone to celebrate it with him. I doubted it. Made me feel profoundly sad for him, living all alone, his own two kids far away, caught up in their own lives. Maybe they planned to call him on the phone, wish him a happy birthday.

Was he going to do anything special to mark the day? A cake? Ice cream? Any cards, or presents? It didn't seem right, especially compared to Tanner's seventh birthday, which we celebrated earlier this month, with much fanfare and pomp.

That night, I discussed it with Alfredo, when he called to ask how the kids' day had gone. After explaining that Tanner had gotten stung by a bee and Jackie had tripped on a tree root and gotten a bloody nose, I went on to tell him about how David had confided in me, while we were in the elevator, that he had a bit of an obsession with calendar dates. I knew that allowing things like birthdays and holidays to come and go unheeded must be especially discouraging for him.

Alfredo agreed that David was a very nice guy, deserving of friends, and that we should go out of our way to make him feel welcome. He even suggested that we invite David over for dinner again, reminding me how much the kids had enjoyed his company when he'd been with us the last time, on Christmas. I concurred, resolving to be a better friend for him. To invite him to socialize with us. It was the least I could do, after all the hurt I'd caused him.

CHAPTER 32

DAVID

February 14.

Nevertheless, to avoid fornication, let every man have his own wife, and let every woman have her own husband.

1 Corinthians 7:2

Super awkward. Ellen's been ramping it up. Making ever-increasing efforts to get my attention. Flirting as though we were still teenagers.

It's more than a little ironic that even though she's single and twenty years younger than I am, I have no interest in her, finding myself increasingly obsessing over a grumpy, sour-faced older woman who happens to be comfortably married to a very nice man. Alas. The vicissitudes of life.

I found, on my desk, a sealed Valentine's card today. Knowing who it was from, I quickly deposited it into my top drawer and didn't open it until after school, not wanting to risk one of my students seeing it. Which was a prudent choice – the card was even more maudlin than I'd thought it would be. Ellen had hand-written a long letter, tucked inside the card. Page after page of excessive sentimentality, a confession of her true love, amid constant suggestions that she would be absolutely devastated if I didn't reciprocate with my own feelings. Groan. I knew I'd have to find a way to let her down gently, and that I would, after that, have to maintain something of a professional working relationship with her for untold years to come.

Super awkward.

On a happier note, there was a text on my phone, inviting me yet again to go to Consuelo's house for dinner. I'd been there several times since Christmas, and this time she said it was actually Alfredo's idea that I come. If that didn't beat all. She also mentioned that the kids have been asking about me.

This relationship has come to border on the bizarre. Why, I have to wonder, am I so comfortable around Consuelo and her husband and children? Why is it that my interactions with Ellen are so much more clumsy and embarrassing? Why do I find myself looking forward to going to Consuelo's house, finding a sense of calm there that seems to have evaded me for my entire life? The old animosity is entirely gone. She definitely can be prickly, but her attitude toward me is exactly opposite to what it once was.

Jake Powell has apparently licked his wounds and gotten over the humiliation of the past. He's up to his old antics, loudly and brashly displaying his superior knowledge, taunting the other students, speaking out of turn. He and Andrew sit there and openly mock their peers, laughing loudly at the crude jokes they whisper to each other.

It's hard to feel any love for those two. I sometimes can't wait for the school year to be over. They're both juniors, but even though they'll be back next year, they won't be in my class. With the summer only a few months away, I find myself focusing on the fact that I only need to hang in there for a little longer.

CHAPTER 33

CONSUELO

February 14.

David and I eat lunch together in my office now, every day. He doesn't seem to mind not being in the cafeteria with the rest of his students. I think he likes being with me, but I know he's also concerned about the propriety of the two of us being seen together so frequently. We're both professionals, and we understand that the proper decorum is for us to maintain an appropriate distance, especially while at our place of work. But no one seems to notice or care that we eat together in my office. Which is totally fine with me, even if it makes him seem to squirm a bit.

Today he showed me the love letter he got from Ellen. He was so embarrassed about it, not knowing how to respond, seeking my advice. I'm glad he's taken me into his confidence, that he trusts me with something like this. The letter was way over-the-top, and more than a little humorous. The last thing I'd want to do would be to hurt Ellen's feelings, though, or even for her to ever find out that he'd shared the letter with me.

We sat there and read through the whole thing together, during our break. I gave him some pointers on the most appropriate way to respond – that he needed to make it abundantly clear that he didn't feel "that way" about her, followed by a list of the traits he truly admires in her, and how he hopes they can continue to be good friends, etc. He seemed genuinely grateful for the help.

Upon completing that task, I moved to a different topic. Pointing at his meager lunch (a can of kippered herrings which stunk up my office after he opened it, and a small apple), I said, "Listen. Old bachelor that you are, you probably don't maintain much of a social calendar. It's obvious you have no interest in spending any time with young hotties like Ellen, anyway. And, since your cooking skills seem to leave something to be desired, as evidenced by the food you've been bringing for your lunches (if it can be called food), I suggest that we set a standing appointment for you to come and eat with me and Alfredo and the kids, once a week, on Sunday afternoons. It'll do you good. What do you think?"

He looked at me with amusement.

"Do you think they'd mind?"

"Of course not. They love you. Let's say, four o'clock. Starting with this Sunday. Deal?"

"Deal," he said, smiling at me. "What do you want me to bring?"

"How about a salad?"

"Can it be the kind that comes in a bag?"

"Absolutely."

"Ok then."

Good. I was glad I hadn't had to twist his arm.

I was surprised to realize, after he'd left, how nervous I'd been to invite him. And how relieved I was when he'd accepted.

CHAPTER 34

DAVID

March 14

If we confess our sins, he is faithful and just to forgive us our sins, and to cleanse us from all unrighteousness.

1 John 1:9

I WROTE A CURT REPLY, in February, to Ellen's love letter. To my relief, she responded well, messaging me on Facebook, insisting that she never intended to embarrass me, and that she hoped we could still be friends. I let Consuelo know about it, and thanked her again for her help.

Today is Pi Day – 3.14. Consuelo made three kinds of pie for dinner tonight, to celebrate. Pumpkin, chocolate, and strawberry.

It's become a regular thing, these Sunday evening dinner appointments. The kids always bring out their board games, and we have a fun time together – *Battleship, Monopoly, Apples to Apples.* Sometimes Consuelo and I play *Trivial Pursuit* together, but whenever we do, Alfredo and the kids drift off. Not their thing, I guess.

Alfredo and I have actually become good friends. He, too, enjoys martial arts, though he doesn't do much with it now. We have the same general taste in music, and we're forever trying to stump each other by citing obscure lyrics from 1970s rock anthems. He's younger than I am, and I think he has a problem with depression. One of these days I might mention it to him. Suggest some sort of medication, perhaps. Or at least a doctor visit.

Sometimes he's up, but other days, he's forlorn, silent and brooding. It's so odd to me that, of all the people he could bond with, he seems to have chosen *me* of all people – the guy who's trying not to obsess on his wife – to become his friend. I don't think he has a lot of social interactions, outside of my weekly visits. He's an accountant for a lumber company which seems to be shrinking in size every year, due to a never-ending string of layoffs and logging restrictions. I can't imagine what he'd think if he knew how much it was killing me to be there at his house every Sunday night, so close to his wife. How many times I've thought about her. How inappropriate those thoughts of mine have sometimes been.

Last Sunday, after church, I met with the leader of our little congregation in his small office, closing the door behind me, to make a full confession of my fixation, including the enormous guilt it was causing me. He advised me to change my thought patterns by focusing on something loftier, to make my obsession a matter of daily prayer, to seek help from God so I could stop harboring inappropriate thoughts. To petition the Lord for strength of character, and to put Consuelo, as an object of physical desire, completely out of my mind. I've begun to do that, and I have to admit that it has provided some measure of relief. At least my thoughts of her are more pure and wholesome these days. It's a start.

But I simply don't have it in me to stop going to her house on Sunday afternoons. Those times with her family have become the highlight of my week. They're what I live for. The thing I most look forward to.

CHAPTER 35

CONSUELO

April 7.

Who would've believed it? Life is indeed stranger than fiction.

The guy who last year was my sworn enemy above all others, has somehow broken through the barrier surrounding my heart. Not fair.

I can't really tell how he feels about me. He does seem to enjoy coming over on Sundays.

And as for all those arguments we had, before that night in the elevator? Just bravado on my part. I was just trying to goad him. Really. It's not that I've abandoned my ideals, but I didn't actually disagree with him all that much, in the first place. I just wanted to argue. To clash with him.

Even his politics don't really bother me. Truth be told, I harbor a lot of libertarian-leaning sympathies, myself. We're a lot closer, in that regard, than one might think.

Lately we've been doing a bit of bible study together. I'm trying not to push things too far with him, in terms of spirituality. Don't want to overwhelm the guy. My personality can come across as overbearing at times, I know. So I'm keeping our studies to just a few innocuous verses from the bible for now, with some non-committal discussion on the teachings of Jesus, etc. I kind of have a nagging feeling that this is the way God wants me to pursue things, at least for the time being, anyway. David needs this in his life, I think. Maybe one of these days I'll feel emboldened to invite him to come to church with us. Not yet. We'll see.

Alfredo and the kids have bonded with him, though, more than I ever thought they would. I find myself feeling vulnerable and excited at the same time. I don't want to be too aggressive or obvious. The last thing I'd want to do would be to frighten him, or push him away.

There are days when I'd swear that he really likes me. But at other times he's aloof, distant, closed. Preoccupied. He's hard to read. Kind of like Alfredo, in that regard.

CHAPTER 36

DAVID

April 15.

*And it came to pass in those days, that there went out a decree from Cæsar
Augustus, that all the world should be taxed.*

Luke 2:1

TAX DAY.

Income taxes – don't get me started.

I got into a discussion with Consuelo about alternative ways of raising
revenues, to replace the federal income tax altogether – user fees,
volunteerism, land value taxes. To her credit, she actually listened to
what I had to say and didn't immediately disagree. A minor miracle.

Consuelo and Alfredo have begun to do a bit of scripture study with me, after dinner on Sundays. Nothing overly pushy or sanctimonious, just some safe stuff like selections from the Psalms or the Sermon on the Mount. It's nice. I've chosen not to let on that I'm already well-versed in those things. I'm not sure what church Consuelo belongs to, and religion can be such a touchy subject. I really don't want to offend them, or jeopardize our relationship. Not worth it. So for now I'm letting Consuelo take the lead, playing along in an innocent way, mostly just sitting on the couch next to the big china cabinet in her front room, listening, making little contributions here and there.

I know her well enough to know she can be hard headed, and the last thing I'd want to do would be to engage in bible-bashing, or debating with her over whose church is right and whose is wrong. And anyway, she seems to interpret the various verses we discuss in the same way I would, so I'm content, for now, to leave things the way they are.

CHAPTER 37

GLORIA

May 4.

May the 4th be with you. Star Wars Day. Yes indeed.

Consuelo changed out the building locks a number of months ago, after that troubling break-in with the stuck elevator. She issued new keys to the appropriate people, and we've been especially careful to make sure they never get placed into the wrong hands.

In spite of that, there's new evidence that someone's been tampering again. The building's alarm was reset twice last week. Someone has the access code, and it has to be one of the people who has keys. Beth, Abdullah, Consuelo and myself.

Sally Ringerton has been back here to investigate, but, like me, she can't come up with a viable explanation. Extremely troubling. What's going on?

Tomorrow I head with the group for Oregon. Fun. Can't wait to get on the bus with Consuelo. This will be the third time we've done this. Almost makes me feel like a little school girl, again.

CHAPTER 38

CONSUELO

May 5.

Cinco de Mayo. A planned day off from school for everyone today, in which a group of flooring contractors are going to install new faux wood flooring in the hallways. A bunch of my fellow church members got together and chartered a tour bus to take us all to Medford, Oregon, four hours north of here, on this same day. Worked out perfectly.

We met this morning at 4 AM, at the parking lot on the south side of the church. The bus looked like a nice one, sitting there with the engine idling as the driver loaded my suitcase into the undercarriage compartment.

There's a very special place in Medford. A big church building – we call it God's temple – where we visit once a year, as a group, to worship the Lord together. This was going to be a wonderful trip. A beautiful day outside. I was totally excited.

I looked around at the dozens of other people unloading their luggage and boarding the bus and realized that our combined Eureka-Arcata church congregations comprised more people than one might have thought. And on this day in particular, we had an especially good turnout. We were a sizeable group. Bigger than last year, they told me, and the year before.

I stepped up into the bus and made my way toward the back, looking for Gloria. Halfway there my jaw dropped, seemingly all the way to the floor. I couldn't believe my eyes.

David was sitting on a seat near the back, looking at his cell phone. He hadn't noticed me yet. I took a deep breath, then strode straight back to him, plopping down onto the seat next to his. He looked up from his cell phone, no less startled than I had been, his eyes wide with an urgent, unspoken question.

"Yes," I told him, suppressing a laugh. "This is my church. Yours too, I take it?"

It was just a one-day trip, but I think it was the most fun vacation of any I've taken in my life. David and I talked the whole time – four hours, non-stop. Laughing, telling jokes, sharing stories of our past lives. I had no idea if anyone else noticed us, or was staring, or wondering. I didn't care.

Gloria sat toward the front of the bus, waving at me after she boarded, then turning to take a seat two rows behind the driver, not wanting to make me and David become a threesome. I silently thanked her for understanding.

Our time together with our fellow church members was priceless. The spirit of the Lord was strong inside that wonderful building in Oregon. We all felt it, as we joined together to worship Him in His holy house.

Afterward we ate a group dinner at a local Mexican restaurant. You'd think I'd want to branch out and try something else. It's not like I've never eaten other things; of course I have. I love spicy Pakistani curries, elaborate dinners of dim sum, good plates of pad Thai, and so on, as much as the next person. But somehow, my heart always finds its way back to *la comida celestial* – the meal of the heavens. I'll never get tired of eating the foods of my ancestors.

The restaurant staff in Medford had set aside a large room for our group, and the food was fantastic. A mariachi trio, with Spanish guitars, went from table to table, singing boleros for tips. David and I kept them coming back, each of us making requests for the old songs we'd grown up hearing our parents sing – *El Reloj, El Andariego, Ella, Novia Mia*. We drank virgin margaritas and ate *ceviche*, followed by *camarones con crema* and *enchiladas suizas*.

The bus ride home was enchanting. Most everyone fell asleep, and I made a valiant effort to keep up my end of the conversation with David, but at some point I could hold out no longer. He gently woke me up, when we'd arrived back at the parking lot in Arcata. I found myself earnestly hoping that I hadn't drooled in my sleep.

CHAPTER 39

DAVID

May 5.

For it is a shame even to speak of those things which are done of them in secret.

Ephesians 5:12

I FEEL SO SHEEPISH.

I should've noticed the signs, long before now. Of course she's a member of my church. How could she not be? She goes to the one in Arcata. Mine is in Eureka. But it's the same denomination, just different congregations. We're both followers of our Lord and Savior, Jesus Christ. Belonging to the same church. How could I not have seen that before?

Everything fits. It all feels so right.

I find myself morbidly wishing for irrational things, now. Like that Alfredo would suddenly contract melanoma, or die in a horrible car crash, or something. Not good.

Believe me, I recognize the source of such thoughts for what it is. Whenever an idea about Alfredo's demise pops into my brain, I quickly chase it away. I'm not proud of having entertained such notions in the first place. But I can't help it. I get down on myself for it, promise myself I won't allow myself to think that way ever again. Then those ideas start coming back – visions of Consuelo's husband tragically meeting some horrific fate at a young age, leaving her a grieving widow – and I'm all at once overwhelmed with the strangest mix of both guilt and hope.

I was surprised to notice, heading back to California tonight on the bus, that Consuelo wasn't wearing her wedding ring. Had she taken it off for some reason? Maybe she'd lost it. I searched my mind, to think back to the time when I'd last seen it on her finger. Definitely in the elevator, when we were stuck there together. But had I seen her wearing it since then? I couldn't remember.

Why wouldn't she be wearing her ring anymore? Had a problem arisen between herself and Alfredo? Was she having troubles in her marriage? I loathed the fact that the mere possibility produced a surge of hope, deep inside of me. Wrong, wrong, wrong.

The trip home was almost magical. We were sitting together in the back. Gloria – also a member of our church, surprise, surprise – sat near the front. The interior lights were dimmed, and it was dark outside. Everyone ahead of us was trying to sleep, so Consuelo and I kept our voices low, trying not to disturb the other passengers. But it was hard to compete against the sound of the engine that way, so we had to speak almost into each other's ear, and every time her head was close to mine, I could smell the fresh scent of her shampoo, and feel her soft hair tickling the side of my cheek. Delicious. Intoxicating.

Halfway home I noticed that I was doing most of the talking. Her head began to droop forward. She would then sway to one side, catch herself, and sit up again. Two minutes later she was drooping again. After going through these motions half a dozen times, she swayed more widely to the side, and her head bumped against my shoulder. It stayed there.

She drifted into a deeper sleep, her head on my shoulder, her hair tickling my ear. I was all nerves, wide awake, exquisitely aware of the feeling of her head against me, her own shoulder shrugging into my side as she unconsciously snuggled and tried to make herself comfortable.

She was warm. She smelled wonderful. It was all I could do to keep from wrapping my arm around her, enfolding her, drawing her in close. This was a particularly intense form of torture for me, and there were still two hours to go.

Making sure no one was watching, I turned to position my nostrils above her hair and inhaled deeply, taking in her smell, enjoying the moment, trying hard to bury my feelings of guilt.

Nirvana and purgatory, at the same time.

CHAPTER 40

CONSUELO

May 6.

I'd had a feeling, for some time now. It was the bus trip to Medford, though, that sealed it for me. My suspicions had been growing for a while. But after getting back from Oregon, I had to find out for sure. I had to know if David was who I thought he was.

I closed my office door, opened up a new browser window, and put my research skills to their fullest use. His background. His family. Where he was raised. I was good at this kind of thing; I knew exactly where to look, and what to look for. Not just Facebook stalking; I went way beyond that.

Forty-five minutes later I had a very clear profile of precisely who this guy was. This guy for whom I'd fallen. It was as I had thought. My guesses about him were correct. He was the very man I'd been thinking he was.

Gloria mentioned to me this morning that she intends to open up to him about certain circumstances from my past, which I've kept buried for most of my life. Things I'd prefer that no one knew about. But I had to agree with her that it was probably right for David to know them, and I don't know that I could ever bring myself to share them with him myself, if it came down to it. So I'm feeling both grateful and horrified, at the same time, for what Gloria says she's going to do.

CHAPTER 41

GLORIA

May 9.

I asked David to come in this morning, early, to meet with me in my office.

"This isn't about your employment here," I began. "At least, not directly."

He nodded, settling back in his chair.

"I have no control," I said, "over what you guys, my staff, do in your spare time. Outside of work. Nor would I want to. And though I've generally been opposed to all manner of romantic entanglements between staff members in the past, I think it's safe to say that all of us, myself included, are really glad to see that you and Consuelo have warmed up to each other so well, in these past months."

I stopped, surprised to see how embarrassed he'd suddenly grown. David was generally calm and self-possessed. At my mention of Consuelo's name, though, his face turned decidedly red, his eyes dropping to the floor, his fingers fidgeting nervously. What was going on?

"Oh, I'm sorry," I said. "I didn't mean to put you on the spot. I have no intention of discussing your relationship with Consuelo here, and I want you to know that nothing about it bothers me, at all. You're both mature, responsible adults, two of the most important members of my team. Two people for whom I have the utmost respect. What you do on your own time is strictly between the two of you. It's really none of my business."

David nodded, still beet red, still looking at the floor, squirming like he was trying to escape from a set of invisible handcuffs or something. It was impossible not to notice his agitation, and I had to comment on it.

"Your body language is telling me right now that you feel like I've just uncovered some great secret. Like I've caught you in the act of doing something naughty. Stealing cookies from the cookie jar, something like that. Red-handed."

He glanced up at me but didn't smile.

"You've got to admit," I went on. "It's becoming fairly obvious. I mean, after all, the two of you eat lunch together, right? Like, every day. You go for long walks. You swim laps together in the pool, after the swim team's done. She even told me you go to her house on Sundays, to eat dinner with her and the family."

This only made him squirm all the more. I couldn't understand it. What cause was there for such discomfort on his part?

"David," I said. "Please don't think that I look down on this behavior. In truth, to me it's wonderful. Consuelo's been my best friend since I was a kid. We were on the swim team together, from junior high all the way through our senior year. She's a year younger than I am, but she skipped seventh grade, so we were in the same graduating class.

"That was all so long ago. Seems like another lifetime. So much has happened since then. The truth is, Consuelo's life has just been such a downer, for so long now. I can't tell you how refreshing it is to see her smile as often as she does, these days. It's like she's got something to live for, now. I could never condemn such a positive influence in her life.

"Anyway, I didn't ask you to come in to talk about that. And it wasn't my intention to make you uncomfortable. Rather, I thought I would take a few minutes to explain a specific part of Consuelo's past, to help you understand her better. I actually told her I'd be having this conversation with you today, and she was good with it. If I'd left it to her, she might never have summoned the courage to tell you these things herself. At this point in your friendship with her, it's time for you to know. I checked with her to verify some of the details, but it's a story that I've discussed with her so many times, I pretty much know the whole thing by heart. Seriously. Like, every detail."

He nodded and looked me in the eye, still saying nothing.

I took a deep breath. This was not going to be easy.

"There's a reason," I said, "why she's a man hater. Why she doesn't wear makeup in public. Why she always dresses in ugly clothes. Her layers. Her frumpy pants. The saggy sweaters. Those awful reading glasses.

"Something happened to her. When she was still quite young. To my knowledge, she hasn't shared this with anyone other than me. At least, not for years. But you've become such a good friend to her, now. You need to know her story. And I doubt she'd ever tell it to you herself."

I took a another breath, letting it out slowly, before continuing.

"You already know she got her master's at Berkeley. She did her undergrad at USC. Chemistry. She and I stayed in touch during that time, though I was on the other side of the world. I actually began my college career with a year-long study abroad program in the UK.

"Consuelo went to USC?" David asked. "How'd she afford it?"

"Full-tuition scholarship," I said, "of course. Plus room and board. Otherwise it would've been impossible."

"No kidding. Academic scholarship?"

"She's smart. As you've already figured out. She was actually only seventeen, when she got in. Graduated early from high school, as I said. So she started at USC in the fall, barely after her seventeenth birthday. Ended up living at a place called Trojan Fields. Off-campus. She had three roommates. One of them, Belinda, sort of became her buddy. At least at the start of the semester, anyway. They began to hang out together.

"The two of them made quite a pair: Belinda, the quintessential beach bum – blonde, fake eyelashes, toenails painted in alternating colors, five piercings on each ear, shorts and tank tops every day of the week – and Consuelo, who was pretty much the polar opposite in every respect.

"But Consuelo didn't want to come across as a prude, or discriminatory, or judgmental. So she went along with it. Went places with Belinda. Hung out with her. At least at first. Dances, parties, stuff like that.

"It only took a few weeks for Consuelo to realize how incompatible the two of them were, in terms of their friendship. They drifted apart socially. But they still lived together, so sometimes they talked.

"A month into the semester, Belinda came home one night with a creepy new boyfriend. Guy who smoked weed like a chimney, tattoos all over his face. Enough nose rings, earrings and tongue studs to add five pounds of weight to his mohawk-shaved head. He wasn't even in college. Just some local loser she'd picked up at a bar somewhere."

"Savory fellow," said David, raising his eyebrows and shaking his head. I grinned in silent agreement, but my mood was too somber to laugh.

"They started spending the night together," I said. "Belinda and the creep. Every night. On the front room sofa. Disgusting. It was like the guy was living with them – using their shower, eating their stuff out of the fridge. The other two roommates were mostly ok with it. They hardly spent any time at home, anyway. But the situation really, really bothered Consuelo. She tried to talk to Belinda about it, but Belinda just blew her off.

"Then one night, when Belinda had gone home to Oregon for the weekend and the other two roommates were out somewhere, the guy came into the apartment, alone. The door had been locked, but he had Belinda's key. He'd used it before; getting in was not a problem.

"Consuelo was on her bed, doing her homework, when she heard the front door open. She heard someone come inside, open the door of the fridge, pop open a can of soda. She didn't give it any thought. Just figured it was one of her roomies."

Even though I knew where I was going with my narrative, I found it hard to continue. I had to stop for a moment. Collect my emotions. David had reverted to once again being his calm, controlled self. No longer ashamed. He looked at me encouragingly, willing me to continue.

"The guy was . . . *drunk*," I said, surprised at how much of a struggle it was for me to get the words out. "Consuelo could tell. By the glassy look in his eyes. And his breath. It wasn't soda he'd been drinking. It was beer. A whole lot of it.

"He came right up to her, next to where she was, on the bed. Didn't say anything. Then, he . . . he jumped on top of her and she tried to push him off and he started pulling at her sweats and she was screaming for him to get off, and . . ."

David didn't look angry, or outraged, or anything like what I would've expected. Instead, his eyes were simply full of pain. Her pain.

"It's ok," he whispered, his voice rough. "You don't need to go on."

I shook my head, taking a moment to regain my composure. I wasn't finished yet. There was more to tell.

"She screamed at him to stop," I said, my voice breaking. "It only made him try harder. She struggled to get away. To push him off. So he hit her in the mouth. Four times. The last time was harder than the first three. He may have hurt his hand, because he cursed, sticking his knuckles into his own mouth for a few seconds.

"Her lip was cut. Swelling up, fast. She could taste her own blood. Her ears were ringing. She felt like she was going to throw up. Too shocked to cry. Too stunned to do anything other than just lie there without moving, while he finished the thing he was doing. When it was over, he just got up and walked out the front door, leaving it open behind him. Not a word to her. Not even a glance. Nothing.

"It was all so overwhelming to her," I said. "So sudden. So unexpected. She felt completely confused. Violated. Ashamed, because she'd been hanging out with that wild girl, Belinda, you know? So she started blaming herself. Thinking that maybe she'd deserved what she'd gotten. Or that maybe she was going to get in trouble with her dad, for allowing it to happen in the first place. Like the whole thing was at least partly her fault, right? She felt so guilty. So dirty. She wanted to kill herself. She wished she was dead."

David turned his face away and looked out the window, eyes filled with anguish.

"She didn't know who to tell," I went on. "She was only in her teens, after all. A minor. Should she go to the police? That thought didn't seem plausible to her until almost a week after the incident. It wasn't until then that she was even able to come to grips with the fact that she'd actually been *raped*.

"She was utterly depressed. Couldn't keep any food down, during that entire week. Whatever physical evidence remained from the attack was bound to be undetectable after so much time had passed, so she reasoned to herself that reporting the crime wouldn't be of any use, anyway. She never filed a police report. Never told anyone.

"Mentally, she was in a state of constant torment. Should she talk to her roommates about it? Her family? Telling me was not an option, even though I was her best friend, because I was in southern England, half a world away. It wasn't like she could just stop by my house and have a good, long chat with me. And there was no way she was going to discuss the thing over the phone.

"Consuelo really had no idea what to do. She was desperate. Devastated. Her dad's an easy-going kind of guy, but he's very religious, and he wouldn't have understood. He would've blamed her. At least, that was what her thinking was, at the time. It was hard for her to keep her thoughts rational. She couldn't stop crying. She didn't want anyone to see her. She hid out in the library every day, on campus, until midnight. Stopped going to her classes. She was afraid to come home, worried she might encounter Belinda's nasty boyfriend again.

"It wasn't until a couple of months later, when she'd skipped her second menstrual period in a row, that she began to suspect that something was wrong. She went to a doctor on campus and was given the worst news she'd received in her life. With no warning. No advance notice. It was official – she was carrying that rapist's baby, inside her body.

"She fainted, in the waiting room, right after talking with the doctor. They put her on a bed and gave her orange juice, patting her gently on the arm, assuring her that the first trimester was always the hardest, that her morning sickness would eventually pass. They had no idea what was really going on inside her head. Not a clue.

"She decided to stay in college. Not to go back home. She wasn't willing to let her family know what'd happened to her. She wouldn't have wanted them to see her later on, anyway, once her tummy began to show. So the pregnancy became her darkest, most closely-held secret. One which she went to great lengths to keep hidden from the world. She signed up, far in advance, for summer classes, determined to continue with her schooling and stay in L.A. through the end of the pregnancy. After that, she'd think about what to do next. When she could deal with it.

"She began wearing baggy clothing. Put on a lot of weight, eating like crazy, trying to escape from the realities of daily life. To bury the pain. All she wanted was someone to confide in, someone who could answer her questions and help her know what to do. But there was no one.

"I'm sure she would've told me about the baby, if I hadn't been in London. A phone call or a letter would've been too awkward for her, though, so she chose not to let me in on the secret. At least, not until later. After I got back.

"Belinda was the only roommate who was ever at home. The other two were never around, it seemed. And Belinda never paid Consuelo much attention, anyway. The rapist boyfriend, by the way, had dropped Belinda like a concrete balloon and skipped town, never to be seen again. No one had any idea where he went. No one cared.

"Consuelo realized, months later, that Belinda, too, had gained a significant bulge in the middle, easy to notice under the tight clothing she always wore. That loser of a boyfriend had gotten her pregnant, too. Poetic justice, Consuelo thought.

"She decided not to tell Belinda about her own pregnancy, though. The two of them weren't close that way, any more. And she was sure Belinda wouldn't understand. She had no doubt that Belinda's pregnancy had been nothing more than the result of not taking proper precautions. Not a case of sexual assault.

"As summer approached, it got harder and harder to keep the secret. Consuelo was looking really fat, under her baggy clothes. She never wore anything even remotely tight, to avoid revealing her belly. Everyone just thought she'd put on a lot of weight. She didn't talk with anyone. Tackled her studies with a laser focus. Avoided any and all social contacts. It was like she was barely alive.

"A government case worker came to the apartment one day, to meet with Belinda. Consuelo overheard the conversation. It turns out that Belinda had decided to claim, even though she was about to head into her third trimester, that her pregnancy was indeed the result of a forcible rape, and that she was therefore within her rights to seek an abortion, irrespective of the state's laws at the time. The social worker said it wasn't her place to make judgements, and that arrangements would be made for outside funding to cover the costs. They set an appointment to visit with the doctor who'd be performing the procedure.

"Someone, maybe Belinda herself, contacted the *LA Times* and convinced a reporter to cover her story – 'rape victim defies convention, insisting on her right to have a late-term abortion.' It came out in the paper, less than a week before the scheduled date of the procedure. She was so pleased – the story took up more than half a page, with several flattering photos and a smattering of lurid details on how she'd been viciously molested. The difficult choices Belinda had been forced to bravely make were presented in great detail, as was the incredible courage she'd shown in daring the state to come after her for taking such a significant stance, entirely within her rights, as she saw it.

"The reporter had, with great sensitivity, provided the particulars of Belinda's story, encased in the framework of a carefully supportive, sympathetic viewpoint. Little was said about the boyfriend's whereabouts, or Belinda's reasons for not choosing to abort until so late in the pregnancy. The publication of the article was timely, coinciding with a widely-covered public debate in Sacramento only two weeks earlier, on state funding levels for Planned Parenthood clinics."

I realized I was gripping my cell phone so tightly my knuckles were showing white. I willed my hand to relax, set the phone down on my desk, took a couple of slow breaths, and continued.

"The very same day," I said, "that Belinda went to the nice doctor to get that little baby vacuumed out of her tummy, Consuelo's own body went into labor. Premature labor. She was all by herself, in her apartment. Horrified. It was raining outside. Her labor pains were unmistakable, but they'd come eight weeks too early. She'd only barely been seven months along, by her count. The contractions kept getting stronger, though. They weren't going to stop. There was no denying that the baby was coming, early or not.

"Completely alone, she nevertheless refused to call anyone or get help. She'd been intending to make an in-depth study of the entire birthing process but hadn't yet gotten around to it, figuring she still had a couple of months to go. Which meant, she was largely ignorant of what to expect, and how to deal with things. And she was only seventeen.

"When the contractions became unbearable, she got up and waddled to the bathroom. She barely made it, slipping and falling onto the tile floor when she got there. After a lot of sweating and uncontrolled pushing and gritting of teeth, she was nevertheless shocked to discover that a tiny newborn body, covered in fluid, was suddenly on his back on the floor in front of her, wriggling and wailing with an insistent little voice that demanded attention.

"She was worried that a neighbor might hear the baby's crying. The urgency of the sound was like a needle stabbing into her, piercing directly into her eardrums. Excruciating. Impossible to ignore.

"So she reached for the little boy to try to calm him, placing her warm palm on his chest, stroking him gently, unable to bring herself to actually pick him up. She reached into a bathroom drawer with some effort and grabbed a pair of haircutting scissors, snipping the umbilical cord. And though she'd been largely ignorant of the fact that there existed something called an afterbirth, she delivered the placenta, anyway. Not much choice in the matter.

"The contraction pains for the afterbirth were worse than the ones that had caused her kid to come out in the first place. Then she threw up.

"She lay there naked on the cold tile, sprawled in her own vomit and blood, terrified of the living thing next to her. Should she try to hold it? Or feed it? She wanted to. She didn't know what was holding her back. It was all too shocking. Too horrifying.

"The baby kept crying, and Consuelo was freaking out, more than she ever had in her life. Hyperventilating. Feeling the dizziness, the shortness of breath. The symptoms of mild shock.

"Not knowing what else to do, she slipped him into a black plastic garbage bag, feeling impossibly guilty over the secret desire lurking deep within her soul, that somehow the little boy wouldn't survive.

"The whole thing felt so unfair to her – Belinda being able to run off and get her abortion done without any undue pain or stress, while Consuelo had to deal with this new life. *Her* baby. *Her* child. She was a mother now.

"But she couldn't shake the feeling that the boy seemed evil to her, knowing who the father was. Even though the baby carried her genes, he also carried *his*. Would the little guy grow up to be a rapist, like his daddy? Her thoughts were clouded by a horrible vision of her boy in twenty years, the spawn of a grossly wicked man, covered with tats and piercings, forcing himself onto one unwitting victim after another. She felt like screaming.

"In a daze, she cleaned everything up and ran out of the apartment, into the rainy night, carrying the plastic bag with her. The baby had become so quiet, she thought maybe it had indeed died, after all. She walked for miles, hardly noticing the rain, having cried away all her tears. Nothing kept her moving forward but grim determination.

"She finally reached a part of town in South-Central where there was an abundance of graffiti. Garbage strewn all over the place. It was amazing that she wasn't accosted or murdered that night. She was in one of the highest crime areas of the city. It was almost as though she *wanted* someone to find her, to beat her senseless and rob her and take away her life. Put her out of her misery. But that was not to be. The steady rain and the late hour combined to make the streets and alleyways largely empty. Just her luck.

"As always, she was utterly alone. On her own. She looked around and found an open dumpster and, without allowing herself to give it another thought, tossed the garbage bag in. The baby didn't make a sound.

"She was dragging herself along by the time she got back to her apartment. She'd lost a lot of blood, I'm sure. Her sweatpants were soaked, and not just from the rain.

"No one was home. She checked the bathroom once more to make sure everything was cleaned up. She stumbled into the shower and threw her clothes into the washing machine. Then she collapsed onto her bed, too tired to sleep.

"Late the next morning, Belinda, cheerful, thin again, happy to be free of her burden, was listening to the news on the TV in the front room. Consuelo, barely awake, overheard a reporter talking about how someone in South-Central had discovered a live baby, crying, inside a plastic bag in a dumpster only hours earlier."

"I think I remember reading about that," David said, his eyes wide. "Made the national news."

"Sure did. Consuelo's fifteen minutes of fame. Except no one ever found out that the baby was hers, of course. She'd been a minor at the time of the rape anyway, so even if they'd known, they wouldn't have put her name out there.

"Be that as it may, a herculean effort was undertaken to save the life of that little boy. Emergency personnel arrived on the scene. Life-saving procedures were employed. An advance team was assembled in the ER, waiting for when the ambulance arrived. And there were news crews, and cameras. Lots of cameras.

"Americans from coast to coast followed the story closely, rooting for the tiny, helpless infant who some wicked mother had heartlessly abandoned in a dirty dumpster.

"A team of doctors worked through the night and into the next day to try to keep that feeble little heart beating. But sometime in the early evening of the following day, the lead physician called it. Consuelo's little boy had finally died."

I had to stop, to wipe away a stray tear. David was looking out the window, his eyes moist.

"I don't know if I can adequately describe to you the things that went through Consuelo's mind on that day. The absolute contradiction of how that initial newspaper article, along with several others which followed after, had essentially congratulated Belinda for making such a 'tough' decision, courageously defying the rules, getting her baby aborted so late in the game. As though she were some kind of feminist hero. And, of course, the follow-up interviews with the medical people who performed the operation, along with the social worker. All of whom were well paid for their services, of course. Congratulated, even. As though they were being collectively patted on the back by society, for contributing to the efficient elimination of a tiny person who'd been completely helpless to stop them from doing what they'd done.

"Contrast that with Consuelo. She'd carried a baby from the same father. She and Belinda had lived together as roommates, and they'd both gotten pregnant, probably within days of each other. But where no one seemed bothered in the least by the deliberate, conscious termination of the life of Belinda's child, Consuelo's own baby, roughly the same age, became a topic of national concern. Untold efforts and resources were poured into the desperate fight to save his life. His passing was considered a national tragedy by millions of people. The story dominated the headlines for days.

"How was she to make any sense of such a dichotomy? What kind of a crazy world was she living in? The absurdity of the situation was devastating to her, psychologically.

"After it all blew over, she underwent a fundamental personality change. From a smiling, carefree intellectual to a world-wise, introverted misanthrope. Without ever really making a conscious choice about it, she ended up changing the way she dressed, the way she acted, the way she lived.

"She pursued the rest of her college years with a vengeance, but after that she wanted nothing more than to escape, to hide, to live somewhere far away from USC and Berkeley. The other end of the state, which was different enough to be like a whole other world.

"She wanted a behind-the-scenes job where she could work in a strong supporting role, but without having to be the decision-maker or the public face of the organization. She wanted to use her brain, but not to be put in a position where she would have to pretend to be happy. Not to be forced to artificially make herself come across as well-adjusted. To have to hypocritically convince anyone that her life was good. Because it wasn't. Most of all, though, she never wanted any man to ever, ever see her as anything more than a frumpy, dowdy spinster, albeit one who was feisty enough not to be challenged. One who was capable of biting off the head of anyone who dared to cross her. Because the wounds of her past were just too painful to ever be reopened."

David was looking steadily at me, sitting upright in his chair, a penetrating gaze in his eye. I sighed and shook my head.

"Consuelo has confided in me," I continued, "that she long ago lost count of the number of nights since that time, when she's woken up in her bed in a cold sweat. It's always the same dream – she's running through the rain with a baby in her hand, and Belinda's boyfriend is right behind her, carrying a knife.

"Not a day goes by that she doesn't wish she could take back what she did. The overwhelming guilt she feels, for the loss of that child. But of course, it's too late. Nothing she can do about it now. What's past is past.

"She never found out what they did with the body. Did they bury him? Or just deposit him into a dumpster somewhere, like she'd done? The little boy had never even had a name. He'd only spent a few brief hours in this harsh world, thanks to her. There was probably nothing wrong with him, physically, other than his tiny size. He'd be in his thirties today, if he'd survived. He'd have a wife and kids. Consuelo would be a grandmother.

"But none of that ended up happening. It wasn't to be. Because, in her view at least, she let him die. She *wanted* him to die. It was a wrong choice she made on that awful day. A bad choice, with permanent consequences. And she knows she can never take it back."

"Stop," David said, his voice sounding harsh. He was frowning. "You've got to tell her to stop thinking that way. She was just a kid. She didn't know what she was doing. She had no support. She wasn't in her right frame of mind. And anyway, everyone makes mistakes. Everyone does things they later regret. We all have skeletons in our closets. We all need God's gift of repentance."

"Yeah," I said, "but not everyone is responsible for the death of another human being. A person who likely could've lived a full life. In Consuelo's mind, there's no pathway to repentance for a person like her. Murder is what some people call the "unforgiveable sin," right? Consuelo sees herself as responsible for someone else's loss of life. It seems to her that the only fair price to pay would be for her, herself, to lose her own life. To make up for what she did."

"No way," said David. "The circumstances surrounding the situation have to be taken into consideration. Any rational observer would minimize her culpability, based on what she was going through at the time."

He stopped, and turned to look directly at the large framed portrait on my wall.

"Anyway," he said, "it would be pointless for her to offer up her own life, wouldn't it? She needs to understand that Somebody already did that for her. For all of us."

A surge of warmth spread through my chest, filling me with gratitude for the truthfulness of the words he'd spoken. How had this good man ended up at my school, of all places? And what had caused him and Consuelo to bury the hatchet between them and to become so close, in such a short period of time? He was exactly what she needed.

Their friendship seemed too significant to be chalked up to mere coincidence. I saw the Lord's hand in it. And the more I thought about it, the warmer I felt, in my heart.

CHAPTER 42

DAVID

May 20.

Whosoever putteth away his wife, and marrieth another, committeth adultery: and whosoever marrieth her that is put away from her husband committeth adultery.

Luke 16:18

THERE'S SO much beauty in the world today, I feel drunk with it.

Numberless yellow wildflowers, strewn all along the side of the highway, waving at me when I pass by, like little golden pagodas, pointing to the sky. Round sorrel leaves, brilliant green, spread among the ferns at the feet of the ageless redwoods, dripping with fog-dew. Sandy beaches, empty of all humanity, with squawking seagulls that spring along the sand on tippy toes, darting among the waves that come breaking in from the endless blue expanse beyond. A deep cerulean sky dotted with friendly puffs of cotton. Busy insects flitting here and there, buzzing about, carrying on like there's no tomorrow. Larks and wrens and sparrows perched in every tree, hopping across the wet lawns, crouching on the rooftops, straddling stoplights and street signs and overpasses.

The whole world, here in northern California, has rebounded from the coldest, wettest winter I've ever experienced. It's a paradise of nature's gifts, now. Gorgeous.

I'm feeling more conflicted than I ever remember being. My heart is tortured by my regular interactions with the one person who fascinates me more than anyone has a right to. The person who (without trying, and apparently without even realizing it) fills me with more feelings of guilt than I've ever felt before. There's nothing I want to do, except to escape into the beautiful panoramas that surround me here, like stepping into a painting, to forget my troubles and lose myself in the blossoms and fragrance and sunshine. With her.

I wish the school year were over.

Going to work would be a chore, except for the presence of a certain assistant principal, who goes for lunchtime walks with me every day now. No one seems to care in the least. But I'm always worried that prying eyes are noticing how much time we spend together, and speaking about it in hushed tones, behind closed doors.

Ellen has long since stopped pursuing me, thank heaven. She hasn't really spoken with me since February, other than to say "hi" when we pass each other in the halls. Jennifer has apparently concluded that her need to mentor me is over. She mostly leaves me to my own devices, which is more than fine with me.

Consuelo and I go swimming together five days a week, after 6 p.m., when the swim team is done using the pool. She's very much a part of my life now, pretty much every day except for Saturday, which has become my least favorite day of the week.

Ever since our trip to Medford, she looks at me differently. I know she's in love with me. I can tell.

About ten days ago, Gloria shared with me what had to have been, without a doubt, the most painful experience of Consuelo's life. Afterward, Consuelo and I went for a long walk together, and talked the whole thing over. I had the chance to tell her, in a gently vigorous way, about the amazing ability of Jesus Christ to heal the very deepest of wounds, to bring comfort to the most tormented of souls, to forgive and forget the most grievous of sins.

I won't relate the details here, of the things Consuelo went through as a young college student – they're far too personal – but I will say that having Gloria explain it all made me come to understand Consuelo, and her quirks, so much better. And it made me love her that much more.

Yes, I love her. Of course I do. I've known that, or admitted it to myself, for quite a while now. But we're both very careful to avoid inappropriate situations, like being alone together where other people can't see us. She always leaves her office door open a crack, during lunch. We're careful not to say inappropriate things to each other. Neither has told the other how we really feel. The subject of Alfredo, and their marriage, is carefully avoided.

Most of all, we never touch each other. That night on the bus, when she fell asleep on my shoulder, was the only exception. I've relived it a hundred times in my mind, since then. That was as close as I'm ever going to get to her. I'll never forget it.

I know that this self-imposed physical restraint is right and proper, in the sight of God. But my inability to touch her is the single thing that drives me more crazy than any other, in this preposterous relationship of ours. Even innocent gestures – a shake of the hand, a quick one-armed hug across the shoulders, a pat on the knee, a touching of the fingers – we avoid these things with a strictness that is both admirable and maddening. I can't help but wonder whether the itch to touch is as strong with her as it is with me.

The absurdity of our situation is growing increasingly bizarre. I have no idea what Alfredo can possibly be thinking, or feeling. Surely he's physically attracted to his wife? Maybe he's gay. I don't know. I've seen them briefly hug, mostly just a pat on the back, but as far as I can tell, they've never kissed. Or anything else. Somehow they managed to produce a couple of children, I suppose, but it seems to have ended after that. There doesn't appear to be any real passion between them. Affection, yes, but not adoration. Not ardor. It's such a hard thing to understand. Such an odd marriage.

I can't bring myself to confront her directly about Alfredo, or her marriage. There's too much at stake. Too much to risk. I don't want to jeopardize the fragile connection between us. It's grown to mean too much to me. It's become a vital part of my life. I'm not ready to sacrifice it. Besides, what would my purpose be? To urge her to leave her husband? Never.

But does she love him? She must. Is there something wrong with their marriage? Something I'm missing? Why doesn't there seem to be any jealousy, or concern? Alfredo obviously trusts her completely. But he must know how much time she and I spend together these days. There are times when it positively feels like she's flirting with me.

And she never wears her wedding ring anymore.

How am I supposed to take that? How does she expect me to respond? I'm completely in the dark. And I'm too scared to do anything about it.

CHAPTER 43

CONSUELO

June 3.

Tuesday. David came over for dinner. I invited him to come, specifically, on this particular night. For a reason.

My discussion with him regarding what happened to me in college wasn't nearly as awkward as I'd feared it was going to be. Now that it's behind me, and David's completely up-to-speed regarding my past, I can see the wisdom in Gloria's suggestion that she tell him the tale. It was for the good, and it needed to happen. There's a reason she's my best friend.

Tomorrow's the last day of school. Finally!

I've never been so ready for the school year to be over. I'm hugely excited for summer break to begin. But I'm not exactly sure how I'm going to keep David in my life, during that time. We won't be seeing each other at school every day.

I know he likes me. I can tell. But I'll admit that it's a bit baffling why he never wants to take the initiative, to move things to the next level. He's been married, twice. He should know about these things. So frustrating. I try to do my best to encourage him, careful at the same time not to come on too strong. I couldn't bear to scare him away, at this point. He's come to mean too much to me. But there are times when he seems so hesitant. So distant. Sometimes I just wish he would touch me. He never does.

I've been on pins and needles, lately. The tiniest things have been driving me crazy – the kids not keeping their rooms clean; Alfredo, complaining about his job again; the dust on top of the bookshelves; Tanner leaving the door open when he goes outside, letting the flies in.

I'd already worked myself into a nervous wreck when the doorbell rang. But the moment I opened the door and saw David's face, a warmth flooded over me. A calmness. My problems simply evaporated into the atmosphere all around me. I stood there looking at him, saying nothing, desperately wanting him to do something a bit risky – to rush forward, take me up in his arms, pick me up off the ground, hold me, twirl me, squeeze me, never let me go.

"Hi," he said, sounding a bit bashful. He stepped inside and walked right past me.

Alfredo came up behind us, holding Tanner's hand, excited by David's arrival, anxious to get the meal started. Per my instructions, dinner was to be served no earlier than 7 p.m., a bit later than what everyone was used to. We were all famished. Which made the food taste that much better.

It was an intimate, wonderful dinner – *mole poblano con pollo, tacos al pastor*, guacamole with chips, *pan dulce*, rice and beans on the side. We drank homemade *agua de arroz* and had an endless stack of corn tortillas to dip into. The table had been sweetly decorated by Jackie, complete with a set of lit candles. So nice.

When we were too stuffed to move, we played a round of *Settlers of Catan* together, after which Alfredo headed off to read a book somewhere. The kids went downstairs to play with their Legos. David and I were, once more, left alone, sitting near each other on the couch by the china cabinet. Close, but not enough to be touching.

I'd been thinking all day about the date – June 3rd – and the significance of it. My heart started to beat more quickly as I glanced outside and saw that the sun had dropped below the horizon. I couldn't help but notice, as we sat there in the living room and talked, that David kept glancing nervously at his watch. Three separate times, in fact, over a ten-minute period. I knew exactly why he was doing that, but I said nothing about it. His obsession with the time on this particular evening only confirmed what I'd already come to discover about him a month ago, when I'd been researching his background on my computer. When I'd learned exactly who he was.

I knowingly looked at the clock on the wall and saw that it was almost a quarter past nine. Time to make my move. I smiled at him.

"Don't laugh," I said, "but I actually need to go take care of something, right now. It'll only take a minute, but it has to be now. Can't wait. And I've gotta go outside, to do it. It's kind of a ritual, I guess. Something I do every year, on this date. Because of a long-ago promise, made to a friend. When I was eleven. I've done it every year since then. Come with me, if you want to. But you have to promise not to think I'm weird, ok?"

I let out a tiny giggle, but inwardly my heart was pounding. I got up from the couch, reached out to him, took him by the hand. He recoiled at my touch at first, but he didn't take his hand out of mine. He got to his feet, allowing me to lead him to the back deck, where we stepped out together, under the stars.

I couldn't look at him. I could only imagine what he must be thinking and feeling, but I didn't want to betray my own emotions. Not quite yet. So I kept looking straight ahead as I led him to the edge of the deck, finding it difficult to breathe. We stepped down onto the grass, still holding hands.

I was shivering as we lay down, side-by-side, on the lawn, looking up into the sky. But it wasn't from the cold. My emotions were raw, open, vulnerable. Ready. Anything could happen.

"I'm sure you must be thinking this is very strange," I said, still acting like I thought he had no idea what I was up to. I released his hand. "But indulge me anyway, ok?"

He said nothing. I couldn't see his face. We lay there for a few seconds in silence, staring at the stars.

"What time is it?" I finally whispered.

He raised his watch to his eyes.

"9:15," he said in a quiet voice. He sounded strained. Tense.

"Exactly 9:15?"

"Exactly."

I let out a deep, happy sigh.

"Then look over in that direction," I said, pointing. "That one star, that seems to be off there all by itself. Do you know which one it is?"

"Of course," he whispered in such a tiny voice I could barely hear him. "That's Polaris. The North Star."

CHAPTER 44

DAVID

June 3.

Let him kiss me with the kisses of his mouth: for thy love is better than wine.

Song of Solomon 1:2

I LAY THERE on my back, on the lawn, staring up into the nighttime sky, with Consuelo at my side.

Finally, I knew why everything had felt so right. Finally I understood.

I lay there with her, gazing at the stars for a couple of minutes, saying nothing, my mind burning. I was too stunned to speak.

All at once, I found that I'd lost a bit of the ability to restrain myself. On impulse, I reached for her hand and took it back, into my own.

She rolled over onto her side and looked at me. I was still staring at the stars, not ready to see her face yet. Which meant there was no way for me to have known that there were tears in her eyes.

A few minutes later we got to our feet. Still holding hands. Alfredo might have come out at any moment. Or Jackie. Or Tanner. I didn't care.

I looked at Consuelo as she wiped her eyes. My face was close to hers, inches away. I couldn't stop looking at her. So beautiful.

"You're *Connie*," I whispered. It was the only thing I could think to say.

She smiled and nodded, too emotional to speak.

How could I have missed it? It felt so obvious, now.

The years had been good to her. Knowing who she was, I immediately recognized the soft eyes, the beautiful smile, the kindness. Standing before me was the skinny little girl who'd kissed me when I was a frightened young boy. It felt as though my family's visit to Ferndale had only happened the day before. I wanted to take her into my arms, hug her close to me.

Before I could, she slipped the palms of her hands up to my face, alongside my ears, shutting out the night sounds of the world around us. Slowly, carefully, her fingertips slid behind the backs of my ears until her hands were cupping them, gently pulling my face toward hers.

Total déjà vu.

Her kiss had the effect of instantly erasing the more than forty years that had passed between us. All at once I was an eleven-year-old kid again, in that old cabin in the forest south of Ferndale.

I'd been married twice, and I'd even had a couple of girlfriends in college, and one in high school. But only once in my life had a kiss made me feel the way I felt now. That had been more than four decades ago, before I'd even reached puberty. But that incredible feeling, long since buried away in some distant chamber of my heart, surged again through my body in a resounding affirmation of its potency, exactly as it had done before. The only difference was that this time, the kiss lasted longer.

My mind was a whirlwind of emotions. Ecstasy. Security. Comfort.

But almost immediately my thoughts began to darken. We'd crossed a major boundary, Consuelo and I. This was so wrong. Soon, I'd have to force myself to release my embrace and be on my way, reflecting afterwards on the wicked thing I'd done, recommitting myself to a life of chastity and virtue and honor.

But not quite yet.

Under the light of the stars in that beautiful place, standing with her on that deck, feeling the magic of holding her in my arms, I simply lacked the will to end it. I savored the moment, committing every detail to memory, knowing that the brief minute or two we shared would be indelibly inscribed into the deepest recesses of my brain, among the most cherished and remembered times of my life.

When we finally drew apart I couldn't look her in the eye. I was burning with guilt. I knew that ours was a toxic relationship which could under no circumstances be allowed to continue. We'd crossed the one line I'd never intended to cross. Her sweet, naïve husband was just beyond the back door, somewhere inside her house.

I resisted the temptation to kiss her again, moving a few feet away from her to be safe. But I wasn't ready to go back into the house yet.

"How long have you known?" I asked quietly.

"Since the bus trip," she said. "I'd had suspicions, before that. But when I saw that you and I belonged to the same church, I knew I'd have to look you up. I found the names of your parents. The places you'd lived. Your last name's different, but I figured it all out. Wasn't hard."

"Yeah," I said. "My dad was an abuser, so I dropped 'Lopez' and took my mom's name instead. When we moved out."

"I think this was meant to be," she whispered, looking into my eyes, stirring emotions deep within me which were best left undisturbed. "You and I. Finding each other, after all these years. We were meant to be together."

"You're saying maybe God had a hand in it?"

"I know He did," she said, smiling. "Without a doubt."

I frowned, abruptly turning to head inside, wondering why God would intentionally have brought the two of us together, given that Consuelo was already happily married. Where was the sense in that? What could the Good Lord possibly have had in mind? But I didn't mention anything about it.

"I guess I'd better go," I said.

"*What?*" she said. "Are you serious?"

"Yeah. I've got a lot of, um, loose ends to tie up. Before the last day of school tomorrow. You know."

I again moved toward the house. She caught up to me and put an arm on my shoulder to stop me, turning me gently to face her.

"David. What's wrong?"

I looked at her briefly before shifting my gaze downward.

"Nothing. I just have some stuff I've gotta get done, that's all. I'll see you tomorrow."

She knew I was lying. So obvious. But I had to have some excuse to get out of there. I was positively on fire with guilt. And desire.

I turned and headed once more for the back door. She was frowning, but this time she didn't intervene.

~

DRIVING HOME TONIGHT, I've come to the depressing realization that I no longer have the option of continuing to live in Eureka.

I love Consuelo, body and soul. More than life itself. But I could never live with myself if I were to do anything to ruin her marriage. Even if that means I can never be with her.

My cell phone, on the seat next to me, just chirped. A text. Probably from one of my students. I'm in the habit of routinely sharing my personal number with the kids in each of my classes, encouraging them to contact me if they have questions or need help with anything. It makes them realize that they truly matter to me.

Sure enough, this text was from Fadila: "Mr. Mendoza, there's something I need to talk with u about. Contact me when u have a minute. It's important."

I glanced at my watch. Almost ten. I wondered what she might need to discuss with me so late at night, on the next-to-last day of school? I couldn't imagine it had anything to do with her grades. Whatever it was could probably wait, anyway. I made a mental note to set aside some time to talk with her tomorrow.

Tomorrow, which will be the last day of school.

And my last day in Eureka.

Because tomorrow night, I'll be packing my things, meeting with a realtor to get my home listed for sale, driving a rental truck to some faraway place. I'll be leaving a carefully-worded letter, making a full confession of my feelings, apologizing for everything, telling Consuelo the truth. That she was, and always will be, the love of my life.

I'll leave no forwarding address.

CHAPTER 45

CONSUELO

June 4.

I knew it.

Not only did I confirm that he was indeed the same David who'd come to my house in Ferndale so many years ago. I also verified that he *loves* me. Even though he didn't say the words, I could tell. From the kiss. He was trembling.

I don't know what's wrong with him today, though. It like he's been avoiding me, all morning. He seemed to be in such a hurry to leave last night, too. Just when I thought we'd finally cleared away all the obstacles, bringing our feelings out into the open. But he took off so quickly, there was no time to discuss any of it. Very discouraging.

He hardly looked at me when he walked past my office this morning. So strange. I've got no idea what's going on inside that head of his. But this lack of communication cannot be allowed to go on any longer. It's not healthy. And I need to know where I stand.

I'm going to confront him on it, tomorrow. At his house. Insist that we talk, that we iron things out between us. No more of this second-guessing, and sneaking around. Tomorrow's the first official day of summer, so we'll have a full day, if it takes that long. To come to a complete, solid understanding.

I know he felt it, when we kissed, as much as I did. No more hiding behind these imaginary walls of silence.

The kids in the school today are bouncing off the walls. I think they're as eager for summer break as I am. They're wearing flip-flops and shorts, chattering loudly to each other, running when they should be walking, looking distracted and antsy.

Fadila just walked by. She looked out of place. Far too serious for a day like this. I hope she had a good year. I know David took really good care of her. But kids can be so mean to each other. I'm glad not to see Jake Powell around. Or Andrew. They no doubt decided to skip the last day of school.

It's not yet lunch time, but someone's making popcorn, in the hallway. Crazy kids. I didn't know someone had put a microwave out there. The strangest things happen, sometimes, on the last day of school.

Who would be making popcorn, anyway, at 9:30 in the morning, out in the middle of the hall? But I can definitely hear the popping sounds. Pop, pop, pop.

Then I hear someone scream.

CHAPTER 46

GLORIA

June 4.

It's now hours after the fact, and many of the details are still unclear to me. An active police investigation is underway, and I've prepared a statement for a joint press conference with local law enforcement, scheduled to take place in less than an hour.

My hands are shaking as I try to type these thoughts into my laptop, but I'm worried that if I don't get this down now, I might forget some of it.

These are the events as they unfolded this morning, to the best of my knowledge and current understanding.

Approximately fifteen minutes after the second-period bell, two males approached the school. They wore heavy jackets and were each carrying a large amount of gear. Their first task was to chain every building entrance shut, so that the exits were all blocked. The chains were padlocked at each door. They entered the building before chaining the final door shut.

Once inside, they moved quickly to the school safety office where Dan, our onsite security officer, was just getting to his feet. The intruders shot him point-blank, in the face and chest. He died almost immediately.

The assailants then entered the janitorial rooms and used a key to enter the elevator control room. They proceeded to disconnect power to the elevator, eliminating that potential escape route. They also unplugged the elevator's emergency phone connection. Then they entered the correct passcode on the door of the electrical utility closet, entered the room, and proceeded to disconnect the school's phone system, the internet, and our backup emergency response plan.

They made various obscene gestures into a number of cameras in our security system, suggesting that they were fully aware that they were being recorded, and glad of it. The fact that they were able to bypass our security codes and had no trouble disabling our systems made it clear that they knew exactly what they'd been doing. They were likely very familiar with the layout and functionality of the custodial area, the elevator control room, and the electrical utility closet. It would've been easy for them to disconnect the school's closed-circuit camera system, but they evidently chose to leave it running, suggesting that they deliberately intended to leave a video recording of their actions.

They headed from the janitorial area to the administration offices, where they proceeded to open fire indiscriminately on any person they encountered, shooting to kill in every case. I was using the women's room at the time, and heard the screams and commotion from beyond the door.

The attackers seemed to operate on the premise of time being of the essence, hurrying to make their way down the first hallway, surprising some teachers and their students in several classrooms, showering everyone with bullets, then moving on quickly to the next room before anyone had time to react. At this point, about three or four minutes into the attack, more than a hundred cellphone calls had been made to 9-1-1, and I believe that everyone in the building was aware of the threat.

People were screaming, running, hiding, pushing past each other. It was utter pandemonium. Complete panic.

I emerged from the restroom to find Jennifer Dahle, the head of the English Department, lying in a pool of blood against a wall, unresponsive. There was a serious wound in her upper thigh. Having had some training in first aid years ago, I dropped to one knee and began applying pressure to the injury. Throughout the ordeal I heard endless shouting and crying, and the distant popping sounds of the attackers' guns, being used on my students. My children.

In my utterly panicked, terrified state, I heard banging on the doors, from outside the building. The police had arrived, finding all the doors locked. One enterprising officer, unwilling to wait for someone to remove the barricade, drove his cruiser directly into the front entrance, crashing through the door, bursting the chains and allowing his fellow officers to enter. They came rushing in, more than a dozen of them, with many more to follow. Their guns were raised, and they were shouting signals to each other, fanning out into the different hallways. None of us knew that the two shooters had already gone upstairs, probably to buy a little more time and inflict greater carnage.

By the time the law enforcement officials reached them, the assailants had already been incapacitated, having been taken down forcibly by one or more of the brave students and teachers in one of the upstairs classrooms. Arrests were made, the building was secured, parents were phoned, and emergency personnel arrived to treat the wounded. The place continues to feel like a war zone.

There's more, but I'm at wits' end, having trouble seeing through my tears to type, so I'll end for now.

This is the kind of day all educators dread. One we hope will never come. I can only imagine the shock and horror each unlucky parent will experience, when that awful phone call comes through, confirming their very worst fears. There can't be anything more horrible.

CHAPTER 47

FADILA

June 4.

I should've insisted. I knew better than to wait.

As soon as I heard the screaming, I knew it was too late. I should've asserted myself. Should've taken Mendoza aside, first thing this morning, and told him everything. I don't think I'll ever be able to forgive myself for not doing that. It makes me feel responsible for what ended up happening.

But I decided that what I had to say could wait, even though today was the last day of school. Even though I came to school scared to death that something very, very bad was going to happen.

I wish I'd been wrong.

Last night, I saw that someone had tagged me in a photo, on Facebook. So I clicked on the link, to see who it was. Which led me to a Facebook page that I hadn't known existed. Totally evil. Freaked me out, big time. Pure hate, against a lot of specific people at the school. Including me.

I knew I had to tell someone about it. To report it, before the page got taken down. It was the kind of thing that gives parents nightmares. So I texted the one person in my life who seems to actually take me seriously – Mendoza. But he didn't reply. He was probably in bed already.

I didn't get to school early enough to take him aside, and I'm ashamed to say I was a little bashful about approaching him, anyway. So I just went to my first period class and sat in my seat and hoped for the best. I figured I'd tell him about it during fifth hour, before class. Bad call.

The shooting started during second hour. I ran out of my class and down the hall, into his class. I'm not sure why. It was like I knew I should've told him about the Facebook page before, and now I wanted to do it anyway, to exonerate myself or something. Or maybe it was just that I felt safer there, where he was.

Enough with the psychoanalysis. The shooters were making their way down the hallway, toward us, stopping to spray bullets into every classroom along the way. Maximum terror. Everyone in Mendoza's room went totally bonkers. Shouting, screaming, pushing each other out of the way, scrambling under desks, cowering in the corners. No one wanted to take a look out in the hallway. We all knew what was coming. Half of us were crying. I stood near a corner along the back wall, waiting. There was nothing else to be done.

The windows were the kind that only opened a small crack – too small to fit through. Someone threw a desk against one of them, but it bounced off and hit a girl in the hip, knocking her over, making her cry. Everyone was squirming, shoving, jostling for position. We all stood there just staring at the door. It was closed. The lock on it hadn't been functional, all year.

Mendoza hadn't joined the rest of us, at the back of the room. He just stood there, in front of the dry-erase board, next to the front door, waiting, like we were, for someone to open it. I noticed that he'd removed his shoes and socks, standing there barefooted. Ready, I figured, to bust some kung-fu moves on somebody.

Everything got very quiet. I could hear the tiny sniffles from the girl behind me. Gerald, with his gigantic shoes, seemed to be a bigger wimp than all of us, cowering on his hands and knees, shaking and crying.

"It wasn't supposed to happen like this," he kept murmuring to no one in particular. "It wasn't supposed to end this way. Not like this."

The door suddenly opened, and two guys stepped inside, weapons raised.

Jake and Andrew.

When the others saw who it was, there was a collective gasp. But I wasn't surprised. I'd already known it would be them. I'd seen the Facebook page. The red crosshairs that had been drawn over the faces of the kids they didn't like. Including mine.

They were dressed in camo hunting vests and pants, standing there in the open doorway with pistols in hip-holsters and rifles in their hands. Their faces were relaxed, all business, locked against all distractions. As if they were in the middle of some kind of intense video game or something.

Jake took one look at me and my heart stopped beating. He made no comment but simply raised his weapon, taking direct aim at my face, ready to pull the trigger. He never got the chance.

Mendoza moved so quickly it was hard to see what he did. His hand flashed out and grabbed the barrel of Jake's gun, jerking it out of the way. The rifle must've been hot to the touch, because Mendoza winced in pain and let go of the barrel, right at the moment that Jake fired off his shot, which went harmlessly into the wall. Before Jake could level the weapon and take a second shot, Mendoza's fist shot at his Adam's apple, connecting solidly with his throat. Jake collapsed onto the floor.

Quick as a wink, Andrew's gun swung around, but Mendoza, anticipating it, knocked it out of the way, grabbing it and wrestling it from his hands. The gun clattered to the floor. Andrew reached for a pistol, drawing it surprisingly swiftly from its holster, but Mendoza's foot swung so quickly that it bridged the gap between them and slapped the firearm out of Andrew's hand. I heard the gun sliding down the hallway floor, outside of the classroom.

For a brief moment, Andrew looked into Mendoza's eyes, and I could see the fear in him. Then Mendoza turned and swung his whole body, three hundred-sixty degrees, in a circular whipping motion, raising his foot up like a pendulum, sweeping the back of his heel across Andrew's face like a windmill. It knocked him over. He was out cold.

Jake, rubbing his throat, started to get up from the floor. Mendoza sent a kick his way as well, bashing him in the side of the face, knocking him back to the floor.

"I need some help here, you guys," Mendoza said, and several of us came forward to disarm our two classmates. We moved all the weapons to the back of the room, and Mendoza stood there, next to me, breathing heavily, looking down at Jake and Andrew.

"Was this, by any chance, the important thing you wanted to talk to me about today?" he asked me. I nodded, unable to find my voice, too terrified for tears.

"I'm so sorry, Fadila," he said, "that I didn't make time to talk with you earlier. I don't know what these guys have done here today, but I'm sure it isn't good. Maybe all of this could have been avoided."

"It's ok," I managed to say. "They're the ones who did this. Not us."

He nodded, but I could see that he was in anguish.

Hasan came running into the room, his face white with shock. We looked at each other but said nothing.

The police arrived moments later, their guns drawn, talking into their shoulder-mounted walkie-talkies. We were all made to stand in a line, single-file, with our hands clasped behind our necks. After a few minutes they led us to a spot outside, on the grass, where we were allowed to wait for our parents. On our way out, down the hallway, we walked passed the body of a kid from another class, lying in blood. I think we were all crying, by this point. I felt something warm on my legs and realized I'd lost control of my bladder.

They made Mendoza sit down at a table in the back of the classroom, where several officers started talking to him, taking notes, writing down everything he said. He seemed distraught, worried, distant. Like he was itching to leave. They kept asking him questions. Finally one of them gave him permission to get up and take a bathroom break. He took off, half-running, passing us on the stairs, taking them two at a time, racing to get to the ground floor.

CHAPTER 48

DAVID

June 4.

Therefore I will not refrain my mouth; I will speak in the anguish of my spirit; I will complain in the bitterness of my soul.

Job 7:11

I SAW FADILA THIS MORNING, before class. I don't think she saw me. I don't have her until fifth period, and I knew she'd been wanting to discuss something with me, but it was time for the bell to ring, so I decided to put her off until then. I wish I'd known then what I know now.

She survived the shooting, anyway. At least that was something.

After I was sure the threat had been eliminated, and that my own students were ok, my only thought was to go downstairs and check on the welfare of the administrative staff. In particular, the assistant principal.

But the place was swarming with law enforcement officers and crime scene investigators who insisted on interviewing me, on the spot. Their questions were endless, and repetitive. I was going crazy. When one of them said I could take a ten minute bathroom break, I didn't need to be told twice. I took off down the hall like a rocket, passing the kids from my own class, who were being marched down the stairs in a straight line with their hands behind their heads. As though they were the criminals rather than the victims.

Near the faculty entrance, Abdullah lay in a pool of blood, face-down. My heart went out to his kids. I knew how devastated they'd be. The irony of their father, having survived the mindless torture and brutality of ISIS in Syria, only to come to America to be gunned down by a couple of teenaged terrorists.

I swung around the corner and burst into Consuelo's office. Her chair was empty.

I breathed a huge sigh of relief. She was safe.

Where'd she gone, I wondered? I thought about where I should go to look for her next. I wouldn't be able to be at peace until I knew for sure that she hadn't been injured. The library? She often spent time in there. Maybe the lunch room? Or the gym? Would she have headed to the swimming pool? Or maybe she was already outside, herded there by the police along with everyone else. Keeping control of the kids, helping with the investigation. That was probably what she was doing. I decided to go look for her outside, on the grass, where everyone else was, for the most part.

I was turning to head off in that direction when I noticed out of the corner of my eye, a shoe. On the floor. Behind the chair.

Her shoe.

My heart was in my throat as I slowly made my way behind her desk.

No.

She was there.

Lying on her side, eyes open, one leg tucked unnaturally back behind her. There was blood everywhere – on her clothes, on the floor, on the desk, on the back wall. How had I missed it before? I'd been in such a hurry, only seeing what I wanted to see.

Her face had no expression. Her eyes were merely staring blankly ahead, as though she were in a trance.

I dropped to my knees and felt her neck for a pulse. Nothing at all. I desperately tried again, in different spots. I rolled her over onto her back and started CPR, going through the motions without thinking, knowing it was all in vain. She'd lost too much blood.

Her skin was still warm to the touch. Soft. But she was gone.

I was at a loss to comprehend the sudden anger that welled up inside of me, as the tears began to spill out of my eyes, dropping onto her frumpy sweater, mixing with the blood. It wasn't that I was upset with the two punk kids who'd done this to her. They'd be getting what was coming to them. Might even be tried as adults. Which, in California, could mean the death penalty.

No, the thing that was making me irrationally mad, as I brushed a red hand across my face to wipe my tears and runny nose, was Consuelo herself. That she'd had the gall to leave me to spend the rest of my time on this planet, alone. Without her.

And she hadn't even had the decency to say goodbye.

CHAPTER 49

BOB

June 4.

What in heaven's name is this sick world coming to? How can people destroy one another like this? How could any person living on this planet be so heartless?

I can't take it anymore. I really can't. To the devil with all my business ambitions for the school, my high-minded goals, my efforts to train the school staff in the ever-revered ways of American commerce. To the devil with all of it. I'm through.

I knew some of them. Some of the people who got killed today. I knew them *personally*. This one hit too close to home. I can say utterly and without reservation, that what happened today was *unacceptable*.

I don't know. Should we simply stop trying to educate our kids altogether, stop putting them in public places, stop herding them into large groups? Are we inadvertently creating something that's just too tempting for those sinister lunatics out there, whose aim is nothing more than to inflict as much pain as they can, and what have you? Maybe we should all hole up in our houses, sitting there with rifles on our laps, keeping a wary eye out, ready to defend our families. What a way to live. What a world.

I'm sick of this. Sick and tired. It's totally unacceptable.

The whole thing has given me a massive headache. How are we expected to go on, after something like this? What's the school board supposed to do now, anyway? How can we be expected to provide words of comfort, solace, or wisdom? It's all for nothing. Futile. Useless. Just a house of cards, toppled to the ground at our feet. Things of this nature.

I'm done. Effective immediately, I hereby resign from the school board. Enough is enough. All that.

Granite, I wish the best of luck to those who choose to remain behind, to sort everything out, or what not.

As for me? I'm outta here.

CHAPTER 50

DAVID

June 11.

And be it indeed that I have erred, mine error remaineth with myself.

Job 19:4

THE MEDIA TRIED to make something of a hero of me.

I despised it.

There was video footage from two different camera angles of my handling of the two shooters. I racked up millions of hits on YouTube. I became the brunt of late-night comedians' jokes, the new Chuck Norris, the self-conscious karate expert who saved unknown numbers of helpless children from two ruthless killers. Radio talk-show hosts clamored to interview me, to ask about my views on issues like gun control and school safety. Single women I'd never met sent emails to the school, begging for my personal info. Claiming they were uniquely and desperately in love with me.

The school board held a series of emergency meetings over the summer. In one of them I was awarded, in absentia, a special medal for valor, or courage under fire, or some such thing. I couldn't have cared less. None of it mattered.

I wished I was dead.

Consuelo's funeral was a national media event. I showed up in sunglasses, standing toward the back, hoping no one would recognize me. I was too upset to cry, unable to pay any attention to the beautiful words which were spoken. Didn't really hear a bit of it. And I absolutely couldn't handle the viewing, so I never even approached the open casket. I just stood there like an idiot, wondering why the good Lord would see fit to allow her to be taken, and not me.

After the graveside service in Ferndale, Alfredo and the kids took a bit of a walk around the cemetery, stealing glances at the assembled crowd. Jackie saw me, and pointed. They headed over. Alfredo's eyes were swollen and red.

"There's gonna be a luncheon, after this," he told me. "At the church. For immediate family, and close friends. I'd like you to come."

Eating was the last thing on my mind. But I had too much respect for Alfredo to refuse the invitation.

"I'll be there," I said.

It was held in the basketball court, in the middle of the church building in Arcata. Tanner and Jackie loaded their plates with cookies and brownies and cake, but Alfredo didn't seem to notice, or care. He and I sat at the table together, picking listlessly at the cold ham and baked potatoes, trying to think of things to say to each other. It was hard.

We both made an effort to steer the conversation to some happier topic, but somehow it always came back to Consuelo. After a while we got tired of fighting it. I told Alfredo what a meaningful person she'd become to me, and how empty my life was going to be, now that she was gone. I wasn't quite ready to reveal that I'd met her at age eleven. Nor was I planning on telling him about the kiss.

He, too, sang her praises as we sat there together, languishing in our mutual sorrow.

"I never would've made it without her help," he said, his voice shaking. "The way she took care of me and the kids this past year, when we needed it most. She was incredible."

"You definitely married a very special person," I said. "She was one in a million."

He gave me an odd look.

"Yes," he said, "I did. But why'd you say that? Because she passed away, you mean?"

I didn't understand why he was asking me that question. *Of course it's because she's passed away*, I thought, but I said nothing. Alfredo kept talking.

"You would've liked her," he said. "She reminded me of Consuelo. A lot. The doctor performed a double mastectomy, but it was too late. By then the cancer had already spread throughout her body. It was . . . devastating. For the kids. For me. I honestly didn't think I'd be able to go on living, let alone continue to be a father. That was when Consuelo offered to take the kids in."

"Take . . . the kids in?"

I was suddenly finding it difficult to breathe. My brain couldn't process the words coming out of Alfredo's mouth.

"Well, yes. She let them live in her home. Move in with her. I've always suffered from depression, you know. But when my wife passed, I was truly at the lowest point of my life. Consuelo was like an angel to us. Exactly what we needed. Heaven-sent."

I shot him a puzzled frown, not at all clear about what he was getting at.

"When your . . . your *wife* passed, did you say?" I stammered, thoroughly confused. He peered into my eyes like I'd lost my sanity.

"Wait a minute," he said, a look of sudden understanding and amazement dawning on him, brightening his eyes. "Do you mean to tell me . . . all this time, you've been thinking Consuelo was my *wife*?"

"Well . . . she *lived* with you, didn't she?" I was trying not to act shocked. Not to hyperventilate. "I . . . I thought she was the mother of your children. She acted like they were her kids."

"They're not," he said. "My wife's name was Rozanne. Tanner's and Jackie's mom. And no, I didn't live with Consuelo. I just spent my Sunday afternoons there, with her and the kids. And with you, after you started coming for dinner. My apartment's actually on the other side of town."

My mind was reeling. None of this made any sense.

"But . . . Consuelo was wearing a wedding ring. I saw it."

Alfredo looked genuinely confused by this. I thought back on when I'd seen the ring on her finger.

"That night when we were stuck in the elevator together," I said, my voice a bit shaky. "It was definitely a wedding ring." I remembered how gaudy it had looked, but I didn't mention that to Alfredo.

Sudden recognition dawned in his eyes. He snapped is fingers as if remembering something.

"Yeah, that was from Tanner," he said, smiling in spite of his sadness. "Plastic. Got it from the dollar store. A week or two before Christmas. He'd been all caught up in the spirit of getting gifts for people, so I let him wrap it up and give it to her early. When she opened it, he made her promise to wear it, like she was married to him. So she did. But only for one day, I think. It must've been the same day you were in the elevator. I think she gave it back to him after that. Or lost it, or something."

I couldn't believe what I was hearing. Consuelo and Alfredo had *never been married.* The restraint I'd been imposing on myself these past months had been completely unnecessary. She must've been wondering, all the time we were together, why I never allowed myself to hold her, or tell her how I felt. And now that I finally knew the truth, she was gone from me. And there was absolutely nothing I could do to bring her back.

"So," I said, carefully choosing my words, "if Consuelo was never married to you, she was just . . . a good *friend* then, I guess?"

"A good friend?" he asked, looking almost amused. "A good friend? David, look at me. I'm *Freddie.* The kid you played with, in the basement, when we built that city out of pillows and blankets, so many years ago. Remember? I'm not Consuelo's husband. She wasn't my wife. And she definitely wasn't just a 'good friend.' Consuelo was *my sister.*"

CHAPTER 51

DAVID

June 3.

For now we see through a glass, darkly; but then face to face: now I know in part; but then shall I know even as also I am known.

1 Corinthians 13:12

A YEAR HAS PASSED, and the pain hasn't gone away. I'm pretty sure it never will.

I've lost track of the number of hours and days I've spent up here on this lonely hillside, among the headstones and grave markers, looking out over the city of Ferndale, and the surrounding farms that stretch across the darkening landscape to the edge of the sea. It's not like I have anywhere else to go these days. And anyway, I've always got plenty to think about, whenever I come here. Especially tonight.

I've long ago given up on trying to stop myself from wondering about what might have been. How things might have turned out differently. It's much easier just to surrender to it, to indulge the whim, to allow my thoughts to turn for the thousandth time to every waking moment Consuelo and I spent together. To engage once more in the futility of fantasizing about what my life would be like today, if she were alive. With me.

THE MEDIA FRENZY died out by the end of the summer, and the school board decided to reopen on schedule, last fall, as a way of demonstrating to the world, and to the community, that we weren't going to allow the shooters to succeed in disrupting our lives. I'm not sure anyone believed them.

A new assistant principal was hired, along with a new director of custodial services and several new teachers. I taught, but my heart wasn't in it.

The school year's done now, and a couple of weeks ago I gave Gloria my notice – this past year will have been my last. She said I'll be sorely missed, but she also told me she completely understood.

The final death toll came in at eight. Five of whom were kids. Another seven were injured, several of them severely. I've visited them all in the hospital. Most of them more than once.

Over the course of this past year, two members of our community who'd been in the school at the time of the shooting have chosen to take their own lives, months after the event, under separate circumstances. A minor, and an adult who worked in the cafeteria. Survivors' guilt. The community has rallied around the rest of us since then, providing publicly-funded counseling and support group meetings. They don't want to lose anyone else to suicide.

I have no intention of following the example of the two who killed themselves. But I'd be lying if I said that there was never a time when I envied them, just a little.

FADILA AND HASAN didn't come back for their senior year. I'm not sure what happened to them, or where they wound up. I truly hope they're ok.

Jake and Andrew are both being held in separate cells in Block A at Pelican Bay, without the possibility of parole, awaiting separate trials. I've written multiple letters to each of them, frankly forgiving them for what they did, wishing the best for them both. If either ever wrote me back, I have yet to receive the letter.

In the months-long investigation and pre-trial hearings, a lot of information came to light which helped answer some of the questions in everyone's minds. Andrew and Jake staunchly refused to respond in any meaningful way to any of the questions put to them in various depositions and interviews, other than to make inane comments such as, "Dude, they had it coming," or, "It was awesome, wasn't it?" In spite of this, the investigators were able to put together a solid, compelling timeline, based on copious amounts of available evidence.

Jake and Andrew had apparently swiped someone's master key – it's still not clear whose it was – and then had driven to Walmart during their lunch hour to make copies, several of which were later found in Jake's bedroom.

Amazingly, he and Andrew had entered the school building, after hours, at least a dozen times during the first half of the year. It wasn't that they had any real plans at that point; they simply found it amusing to venture where they knew they shouldn't, enjoying the challenge of erasing their tracks each time, doing it in so thorough a way that no one could possibly know what they'd been up to. Three or four friends of theirs, whom they'd taken into their confidence, later testified that the two of them had bragged about what they'd been able to do inside the school at different times, with no one being the wiser.

They had, for instance, broken into the electrical utility closet, where they'd experimented with shutting the power on and off, tinkering with the internet connection, resetting the building's alarms, and manipulating the security camera system. They'd been able to gain access to that room by correctly entering the punch-code on the door, after reviewing the high-definition surveillance video footage of Abdullah. He himself had entered the code many times, unaware that anyone with access to the video could, by zooming in, easily see what numbers he was typing.

They'd entered each of the administrators' offices, hacking into their various computers, editing the security camera feeds to remove any trace of their own entering and exiting of the building. They'd considered trying to manipulate their own grades but had thought better of it, choosing to err on the side of precaution.

Their one mistake had been on the day they'd entered the elevator control room inside the janitorial area before the Christmas break, toying with stopping the elevator and disconnecting the emergency phone line inside of it. They wanted to make sure, after locking their victims inside the building, that no one would be able to escape via the freight-loading ground floor exit in the back. They wanted to know that they could, when the time came, disable the elevator.

In the middle of their activities, the alarm on Jake's phone had gone off. He'd forgotten to let his dog outside. If he hadn't headed for home and to take care of it immediately, the mutt would've had an accident on the carpet, and Jake would never have heard the end of it from his mom. Especially since it was only six days until Christmas.

In their rush to cover their tracks and make a hasty exit before driving home, he and Andrew had completely forgotten to reconnect the elevator phone and restore power to it. They had no idea that Consuelo and I were stuck inside.

Jake didn't even think about it until two days later. By the time he and Andrew had gotten back inside the building, they could see that someone had already been there. The phone line had been reconnected, and the power to the elevator was back on. They realized with chagrin that someone was onto them.

After that, to add insult to injury, the school decided to rekey all the master locks, in the first week after the holiday break. It had taken almost three months for Jake and Andrew to find opportunity to get that new master key copied. And the clerk at Walmart had refused to do it for them, because "Do Not Duplicate" was clearly stamped on both sides. So they'd had to bribe one of Jake's lowlife friends, whose father was an opioid-addicted maintenance worker at an apartment complex in the Myrtletown area, to get him to make copies on the key duplicating machine in his dad's workshop.

The most disturbing thing, though, was what Fadila had uncovered, not on Jake's Facebook page but on Andrew's, the night before the incident. Because while Jake was the wise-cracking, obnoxious, outward face of the duo, Andrew was the behind-the-scenes mastermind. The one who was truly, deeply disturbed.

Andrew had kept his page hidden to public view, available only to a few close friends, until the night before the shooting. Late that night, he'd deliberately switched to public view and then posted some additional messages to his timeline, which had alerted the few people he'd tagged who still happened to be awake and on their devices. Including Fadila. It was as though he'd wanted to give his prey a bit of a fighting chance, hours before the hunt, so he'd feel like his 'victory' had been more fair. More meaningful.

Unlike Jake, Andrew wasn't a racist. He wasn't political. He didn't care about causes, or justice, or anything else. He was an equal-opportunity murderer.

He'd been snatching up firearms and military gear from people on Craigslist for a year and a half, amassing a collection large enough for him and Jake to tote multiple weapons of various kinds on the day of their assault. Both had been wearing bulletproof vests at the time of the shooting. Both had spent many hours practicing with targets in the river bar area, on the dry side of the Eel, below Loleta.

Andrew's Facebook page provided endless fodder for the psychologists and social scientists to sift through, theorizing as to where society had failed, and how similar personality disorders could be identified, and stopped, before future shootings like ours took place.

There were dozens of profanity-filled, lengthy essays on the page, detailing everything that he thought was wrong with the world. He ranted about inconsequential things – how his iPhone didn't work like it was supposed to; the fact that a lady cut him off in traffic one morning; that his chicken patty from McDonald's was undercooked once; the degree to which he was incensed at having to pick up his neighbor's dog droppings from his front yard; and so on.

His natural shyness in public was due in part to his significant hearing loss from years of listening to death metal bands for hours at a time through his $400 noise-cancelling earbuds. He binge-watched slasher movies on Netflix and Hulu, sometimes for days on end, and his remaining hours every evening were devoted to his favorite first-person video games: *Hatred, Agony, Manhunt 2, The Punisher, Postal 2, BioShock*.

Andrew was an only child.

His parents had decided it would be best, when he was still very young, to assume an attitude of allowing him to learn for himself, leaving him to either suffer or benefit from the consequences of his choices, without interference from them. To their pseudo-intellectual friends, it had sounded like a reasonable and effective approach to parenting. In reality, it became a way for them to indulge their own selfish whims and desires without ever having to invest any real time or effort in the raising of their child.

They were largely unaware of his activities, providing him with a nearly unlimited monthly allowance and congratulating themselves for allowing him the space and freedom to explore the world in his own way. His job was to learn, through his own decisions, how to get on. They didn't view this approach as neglect; after all, their son had a closet filled with the latest designer clothes, a mansion of a house to live in, and access to all the funds he'd ever need. In their eyes he was a normal teenager, stable, with a consistent social circle, good grades, and a typical, if quiet, outlook on life. They had no idea.

Andrew was, in his heart, a sadist. His private posts on Twitter and Instagram explored, in graphic detail, various means of torturing other human beings. Specific human beings, with names. People he knew. He described with anatomical precision his own fantasies of dismemberment, cannibalism, and the deliberate prolonging of pain and suffering. It was an obsession. It fed a perverse need.

He began to plan the attack on our school when it was late in the spring. Jake, who'd been rejected by all five of the Ivy Leagues to which he'd applied, was already feeling particularly bitter about life when his best friend approached him. He was an easy sell. Andrew had a gift of being extremely persuasive, when he so chose. In offering his plan to Jake, he referred to Eric Harris and Dylan Kiebold of the Columbine High School Massacre fame, to instill a sense of excitement into the unwitting dupe of his scheme.

"It's gonna be like the ultimate video game," he'd said. "Better than anything a computer programmer could come up with. Because it'll be *real*. Totally awesome. Nonstop adrenaline rush. Life and death."

The plan was to finish off the event in an extended shootout with the police, ultimately either getting killed in the crossfire, or taking their own lives. Jake had no problem with that. He'd already decided there wasn't much left to live for. Ending his life at this point was probably a good idea, and getting a mega adrenaline rush at the same time would be just the thing. His only concern was to make sure Andrew had made every calculation to maximize the body count. After all, why go out in a blaze of glory, unless your name could become immortalized along with it?

In the end, the number of people they'd managed to kill was high enough to cause a bit of a national uproar, but it didn't put them at the top of any list of notoriety. Other shooters had taken more lives. And the news media mostly avoided using their names, usually referring to them simply as the EAST school shooters. In a few years they'd mostly be forgotten, left to rot away in prison for decades to come, long after anyone still knew, or cared, who they were or what they'd done. So much for immortality.

Our city and our school dominated the news cycle for a couple of weeks. The usual debate over gun control raged once again, and I was begged many times to participate in talk show interviews, magazine and newspaper articles, and even a book deal. I refused every offer, which made me even more reclusive, and therefore more intriguing, in the eyes of the media. My entire life was studied, scrutinized by people I'd never met. Past friends and neighbors were interviewed, to see what they might say about me. My yearbook photos were uncovered, my Facebook page was scoured for clues, and photographers hung out on my street, waiting for me to go by, hoping to get a candid shot before I ducked inside the house, or my car.

In spite of an absolute lack of encouragement on my part, my story grew into something of a legend – the mysterious, self-sacrificing teacher who put the lives of his students above his own, risking everything to subdue the evil school shooters. Whatever. The news media had been wanting their story; they had it.

⁓

THE SUN HAS NOW DROPPED out of the sky. A bit of a chill has covered the land, even though it's June. I can smell the briny air, drifting in from the ocean.

I'm glad to be alone here tonight, next to Consuelo. As I glance over at her headstone, I can't help but think about what might've happened if I'd actually taken the initiative to write her a letter after that momentous visit when we were both eleven. Would we have stayed in touch? Would we have gotten married eventually, even? How different might everything have turned out? Who can say? At a certain point, dwelling on the past – obsessing on it – becomes counterproductive. I know. I know.

I'm in constant awe, though, at how profoundly she's touched my life, even though I really only spent about half a year, in total, with her.

It's after nine o'clock now. The moon's out, peeking from behind a cloud. I can see Jupiter and Venus, along with a handful of stars. I wait patiently until the moment arrives – 9:15 – and then I slide down from the bench and lie on my back, one hand on her grave marker, my eyes looking up into the evening sky.

The North Star. Constant. Never-changing.

Could it even be possible, I wonder, if Consuelo, wherever she happens be at this very moment, just might, perhaps, be looking at this very same sky? At the same star? She made a promise, after all. And I'm inclined to think that she's just the kind of person who's headstrong enough to make it work, no matter where she is, or what the circumstances.

It comforts me to believe that we're sharing this moment with each other, somehow, in real time. That for just a minute or two, we're actually joined together once again, she and I. I can almost sense her presence, on the grass next to me. It feels like she's holding my hand once more.

No doubt my brain is just playing tricks. But I don't mind. I like it.

After a few minutes the moment passes, and I slowly rise to my feet, standing next to her grave, looking out over the horizon.

My life is far from over. I don't have much, anymore, but I still have some things. I don't have a wife, but I have my own two children. And a new granddaughter, which is thrilling. I'll be visiting both of my kids and their families in Philadelphia, later this year. Can't wait.

I don't have Consuelo, but I still have her kiss. It never takes any effort on my part to remember the electricity of it, to relive the magic of it. I know I'll never lose that.

And I have my other memories, as well. Along with a couple of photo albums Alfredo shared with me, which I've spent hours studying and memorizing. Besides that, I've got Alfredo himself, and Jackie and Tanner. They've become like family to me.

I introduced Alfredo to Ellen a couple of months back. They've started seeing each other, and Alfredo's been teaching her about our church. I'm encouraged for both of them. Life's too short for young people who've lost their lovers to go on living alone. I honestly hope they can work something out. That it'll bring them happiness. I'll be glad for them.

But even as I smile at the thought, I know that nothing like that is ever going to happen for me. I've been through the ringer, multiple times – two wives, a handful of girlfriends, and one true, lifelong love. There will never be anyone else for me. I'm done.

Standing here on the side of the hill in this old cemetery, I say goodnight to my sweetheart. My darling. The woman who changed my life with a kiss. I thank her for everything. I wish her every happiness, wherever her soul is now. I tell her I can't wait to see her again. To be with her. To hold her hand in mine.

I think back on the many good times we had together, smiling as I remember how powerfully she hated me at first. I reflect on the fortuitous timing of the broken elevator incident, how our time together in that confined space succeeded in breaking down the thick layers of ice between us. I marvel at how miraculous it was that, after being apart since age eleven, for so many years, fate had somehow brought us back together.

I see the Lord's hand in all of it, and I'm content.

Finally, reluctantly, it's time for me to leave. I kiss the tips of two of my fingers and touch them to her headstone, uttering the three words I'd never actually gotten around to telling her in life: I love you.

I make my way down the hillside, back to my car, ready to head home.

Tomorrow will be another day. The sun will come up. I'll shower and get dressed. There'll be bills to pay, groceries to buy, phone calls to make, chores to do around the house. Ways to keep myself occupied.

I can't just give up, or quit trying, after all. Because I just might live to be a hundred. I'm fairly healthy, and I have good genes. Who knows?

And if I do happen to reach that ripe old age, I know exactly what I'm going to do. I've known it for years. I'll head down to my old neighborhood, just north of the Port of Los Angeles – Wilmington – and seek out the city park by the Banning Museum. I'll carry a shovel with me and head straight back to a certain corner, which, after all these years, I still haven't forgotten. I'll start digging until I uncover an old jar. One that will have been buried in that spot for longer than most people on the planet will have been alive. I'll open the lid and breathe in the perfumed, ninety-year-old air, carefully unfolding the paper contained inside, reading once more the inane, grossly misspelled prose of an obsessed, ten-year-old romantic.

And that's not all, of course. There are lots of other things to live for, when I put my mind to it.

This summer, for example. I'm going to take the time to methodically explore the woods south of Ferndale, looking for a certain place, a long-ago shared secret, a tiny basin hidden deep beneath the trees, just past the edge of the endless sorrel, which I'm pretty sure no one else in the entire world knows about. An unobtrusive spot where a cabin once stood, now in ruins. A magical place where, as an eleven-year-old, I once found myself standing next to the prettiest, most wonderful girl I'd ever met, and she and I spent an unforgettable day together, talking about what our lives were going to be like, when we grew up. And she'd kissed me.

I know it might take me all summer to find the place. Or longer. After forty-three years, my memory isn't as reliable as it once was. And it's not like anyone else is aware of it, or can tell me how to get there. But I don't care. I'm kind of glad it's that way, in fact.

If nothing else, I've got plenty of patience these days. Patience to find the site that's been haunting my dreams for more years than I can count. A place so hidden away that it might require a great deal of effort on my part to locate it. A place just for me and her, no one else.

Even if it takes the rest of my life, I know myself well enough to know I won't stop looking, wandering through that endless sea of sorrel, until I've found the edge of it. The place where it ends. When I finally do, I'll pause for a moment to close my eyes, savoring the memory. Then I'll open them again, climbing carefully down the natural stone steps into the miniature basin below, concealed by the dense trees and undergrowth surrounding it.

I'll push my way through the thick wall of western sword ferns in front of my face – assuming they're still there – and emerge into the tiny hollow which quite possibly won't have been visited by another human for more than forty years. I'll see the old cabin, likely even more dilapidated after all this time, and I'll step inside and look for the old, familiar, still-remembered items: the loose bits of broken pottery, the mildew-covered books, the porcelain baby doll that was missing its head, the fireplace poker, the three-legged table, the rust-covered stove. I'll glance into the corner where the sewing table was supposed to be placed. I'll look at the wall which had been designated to be the future location of the china cabinet. She'd always liked china cabinets.

Then I'll head toward the big log on the back wall to see if there's anything left of the old inscription, carved so many years ago by a couple of eleven-year-old hands wielding sharp stones, a timeless message etched deep into the ancient wood: "Connie + David," surrounded by a heart, with an arrow poking through it.

I'll smile, closing my eyes for a moment, stretching my arms in satisfaction, breathing in the clean forest air, remembering how wonderful it had been to be a child.

And maybe, just maybe, if the Good Lord is willing, when I finally do return to that unforgettable place in the woods, I'll discover, once I get there, that I'm not alone.

Maybe I'll come to find that Connie's there, too, after all. That perhaps she's been there all along. Standing inside that old cabin, restlessly stamping her foot, waiting for me.

With her arms outstretched.

And then I'll know that I've finally come home.

THE END

www.ingramcontent.com/pod-product-compliance
Lightning Source LLC
Chambersburg PA
CBHW022108240626
47153CB00007B/2282